A-Ma
or Playing the Glass Bead Game with Pythagoras

Content

PLAYING THE GLASS BEAD GAME WITH PYTHAGORAS	4
RUBEN	36
FATHER BENEDICT'S ROUND TABLE OF SOLOMON	49
A MAN TRAINING TO LOVE	82
AMA'S MOTHER	96
CHRONOLOGY OF A MINOR FAMINE IN 17TH CENTURY CHINA	107
A MAN TRAINED TO HATE	145
A MAN TRAINED TO KILL	153
LILITH	181
A MAN TRAINING TO BE	195
VITRIOL	200

...by plunging into the depths of the mind, for which there is no great need to open the eyes to the sky, to raise the hands, to direct the steps to the temple, nor sing to the ears of statues in order to be the better heard, but to come into the inner self believing that, God is near, present and within, more fully than man himself, being soul of souls, life of lives, essence of essences: for that which you see above or below, or round about, or however you please to say it, of the stars, are bodies, are created things, similar to this globe on which we are, and in which the divinity is present neither more nor less than he is in this globe of ours or in ourselves.

Giordano Bruno

Playing the Glass Bead Game with Pythagoras

"She is a witch!"

Whispers disturbed the building silence netting frames of ghastly images on the streets of Macao.

"What do you mean a witch?" that is Ama! "They have arrested Ama!"

This little commotion of confused words, unsettled thoughts and scattered feelings was happening on the streets of Macao in China, sometime in the mid-17th century, during the Age that is known as the one of Reason.

Two shadows, deeply moved and connected in an invisible hug, rushed through the night talking, merging their forms with the moonlight and shadows of the buildings and trees.

"Just after the death of her father that retched soul, Fra Thomas, couldn't settle down, he was the one to arrest Ama." stuttered the ghostly figure.

"Arrest! That is absurd!" The second man shook his head with the most sincere and spontaneous gesture of anger. "Her father is the founder of our Church and University! Their friends are influential, they would not let this happen. When did it happen?" His voice like a bird shot through the wing could not rise.

A family of bats hung upside down observed the scene. They formed a shape of a butterfly carved in rare white jade, the mother whispered silently to her lover:"let us sleep, it is that time of the day…" Trusting her fate to her new just found friend, balancing in mid-air, she opened her eyes and instinctively moved closer to the fire to hear this story, for a story-teller of the bats she was, so she was curious.

Illuminated, in the starlight, their faces narrated an excitement for the tale that is about to begin.

Together harmoniously all the bodies gathered the wood for fire, lit it and let it glows through the night of dancing sadness under the stars, a dance choreographed by the moonlight a thousand of years ago. A shimmering halo like golden desert sand reflected past, present and future, an oracle of thoughts burnt in the fire that very moment.

"Last night! If it happened to her, it can happen to any one of us! Does Ruben know?"

"Ruben? Ruben is nowhere to be found, lost, gone..."

"What do you mean gone? Maybe the same people killed him?"

"To call infinity a number," the bat contemplated "does not make it one."

A restless crowd they were before they were fed and entertained by spirits, later surrounded only by birds, after their fears were lessened, it takes no reading of the stars to see that the men were friends with Ama. Free from death for one immortal moment they sealed off their destiny in the totality of Now.

On the other hand, for the Lord of Death, nothing was too soon or too late, for each soul that has attracted his grasp, only knew about "too late".

"No, no! The two are not connected. He left the Monastery, went into seclusion, and then disappeared a couple of months ago. What bad timing, it is now that Ama needs him the most..."

For several heart beats they just stared at each other realizing how tricky some of their games were, escaping, just in time, the bad ending.

Time entered a spiral of a blazing comet, from past to future, across their lives canvases drawn by ants, insects, bees during just one life-time, with a complete focus on a detail called - destiny. Suspended in one moment we were able to execute wonders. Diving into a brief, spontaneous dance, the bat chuckled to herself, echoing the movement of the stars. Bare-foot, through the woods, to the sea, where it was deep and calm, she listened to the sound of AuM altered by grass-hoppers and frogs. Gathering fruits, berries, healing herbs, she shared her offering with the forest fairies and other restless spirits.

"Fra Tomas is a crook! He is a haunted soul! He hated both of them."

Many more unspoken words of fear, confusion, disbelief, for a moment of eternity, crafted a thick wall of silence. The sound of a bird or wind blowing their way, started the conversation again.

"Ama's Chinese friends will not let this happen... Wait and see..."

"There is no time left to waste. To accuse a woman of being a witch, an inquisitor needs only two witnesses and the confession that is forced out of the accused. I've seen neighbours accusing each other, locking relatives or close friends, punishing the innocent, and often the whole scary witchcraft story is based on the fanciful accusations of scared children."

"Ama would never confess to such a ridiculous thing!"

"I pray that we never come to the moment of trial and notorious enquiries. It is easy to force anybody to confess: pricking her body with needles to find a place, made by the Devil that is insensitive to pain. Do you remember those horrid jail chamber chairs? Full of spikes? I've seen them many times. Poor women either die during the torture, or confess anything to the confessor. Even a thought of the horror of such methods makes me sick..."

"Enough, enough, that won't happen. That is ridiculous! How barbaric can a man be! We are in China! These horrors happen in the main-land, not here! The Chinese wouldn't allow mass murder of their sisters and wives to eradicate flying monsters that supposedly devour children. They are too scared of the spirits of dead, and too civilised to even dream out loud such a nonsense."

"We must help her... We have to act..."

"Fra Thomas is crazy, you never know what he might do next, can we call Father Benedict?"

"He was arrested too..."

"Arrested? For Christ's sake! To arrest an old wise man? This won't come to any good!"

Stalagmites meeting stalactites, inside the caves of the Tibetan or Serbian or Ancient Greek's mountain ranges were the same as the ones in China.

The dark marble with no artificial light, avatars of metamorphosis, inviting in only the bravest, only with the purest of the hearts, for the others will choke within own fear. Plunging deeper in, all myths became reality, all forms merge with divine, inviting Bronze Age rituals of singing, dancing, praying. Deep inside caves, inside the Mother's womb itself, the Maltese Hypogeum or Ethiopian catacombs, with no air, pulsating quicker, drumming, praying, chanting, further opening, further transforming, from Yang to Yin states of consciousness, into the female intuitive brain, as used by Orthodox Christian Priests in Mountains' Monasteries, or Yogis in India, or by New Zealand Maoris, Arabic Sufi meditators, Kenyan Masai hunters, or Australian Aborigines' desert's dwellers.

Personally, passing the Universal black hole, getting transferred into different states of consciousness, with a stone in my hands, rubbing it gently, multiplying the light, singing Kirya Si, Kirya AuM, Kirya DŽ, voices wheedled, the moment stopped, the story teller became real -

"One camel paced meditatively through the desert sand or was it indifferent towards the goddess story about to be born..."

A long, long time ago, somewhere in the higher altitudes of Europe, the ancestor's spirits and the Goddess were allowed no more. No Lady Moon, no Shakti dance, no supreme Taoist exchange of Love, no Bull worship, no scripts to share, no music, no art, no Cobras stare, for 2,000 years the women are put to shame. A shop cat yawned, cats are allowed, as long as they are not black!

Remember, Ama's head was always held high, the memory of her face lit in the glow of the sun-set, "we will hide it in a pomegranate, in the number of 1 and 8 that are no numbers but entities, in our own Strength of Being. We will hide it in "X" and "Ð", in "H" or "Š", inside the numbers of 1,0000 (four not three zeros were used by Ancient Chinese and Ancient Greeks)." Ama wrote it on the stones.

If history is a story, than whose story becomes history?

Asked a man calling himself Pythagoras, guiding his camel through the sand dunes.

Coming from Europe and his future, my reality was Roman, Paris was built by Romans, Barcelona was built by Romans, Belgrade, the city I came from, was built by Romans. The totality of my knowledge was painted by this invisible force that identified itself with an Empire that at the time of no travel, wild mountains, a few cities, has left its stamp everywhere.

Do you read mythology, there where you come from, in the future? Asked Pythagoras during our cosmic encounter while we were playing the Hesse's game of glass pearls, at dawn, during the night of All Souls, in between reality when I managed to jump through the portal that connects all the souls living on our little planet.

A myth is a story that speaks of a mix of truth and lie at the same time. It is like a history lesson from a market place that is at times deliberately exaggerated, to be amusing and teach a lesson. Its ground is maybe real history, only changed to be remembered with extra added facts that were rumours made up on purpose. In very ancient China, wondering monks of 500 AC, collected and transmitted books on miracles of the Bizarre, reporting events from the past, mixing natural with super-natural, twitching slightly so the Real-World encompasses the sphere of Angels, Spirits, Goblins, and Divine that is in its essence intangible. Said Ama's spirit, dancing through the air, as though this type of storyy needs to be danced not narrated.

The whole point of history, you might argue, is its truthfulness, yet when transferred through the poetry, it becomes storytelling and as such carries totally different wisdom. Whispered the bat.

The world of transformation was always associated with the python, or dragon, or snake, so skilfully shedding its skin. Can you sense why my name carries the sounds of Python, God Ra and iSiS - smiled Pythagoras

What about the City of Rome and the Great Mother, I asked.

It is in the nature of humankind to tell stories, and at the root of every culture we find myths and legends. A Hellenistic myth considers Rome to be an Ancient Greek city, narrating a story of a Hellenic Gods and Goddesses. The city of Romolo e Remo, Venus and Mars, cats and dogs, the centre of the original conflict of a female Goddess based worship and a male God dominated rituals.

The story goes back to the Ancient Greece and the Great Mother who has all through the ancient history had a role of the Creator Goddess. Shakti if your wish, with her Kundalini force." Said Pythagoras

What about the famous symbol of Rome, the famous mystical wolf, the symbol of Rome and the twins' brothers?

Lupa Capitolina: she-wolf with Romulus and Remus was cast in bronze during the 13th century AC while the twins are a 15th-century addition, but every myth has the truth hidden within, just read the original... Suggested Pythagoras.

"Shame! Shame! Not in here though, not in Macao..."

Trying to deeper investigate the atrocity of the witch hunt, examining the craziness of some of the Church officials during these times, we came across an official record naming one hundred thousand women with a name and a birth-place killed during these procedures. One hundred thousand women with a name, back in time, will naturally become a scary number of millions of the ones that were un-recorded, too poor to be noticed, too innocent to be noted, the number confirmed within the unofficial rumours of the sane, centuries later.

How the hell it has all began?

Hunted by dogs of own desires, kept awake by own sinful thoughts, Pope Innocent the VIII has decided to blame his sleepless nights on spells and folk magic, punishing all the Mother Earth followers, Devil's worshipers, nurses healing sick with herbs,, single widowed women seducing man in their dreams; the village youth, and of-course the daughters of rich merchants, whose fathers were not to be black-mailed. Supported by Malleus Maleficarum's Witches' Hammer, in its blind madness, the Inquisition got all the power to act against this so-called evil - the hunting manual, printed and re-printed many times in the centuries to follow.

This wicked book was created by the Devil speaking through the two German Dominicans.

This legal slaughter and torture manual became an oil in the lantern of the witch hunting-craze. A best-seller, a hit amongst different classes, passed from hand to hand, read aloud in Churches, and village squares, stored in special places, with the Bible and consulted in the dark corridors of the torture chambers. The best Hunters, and kids would know it by heart, reciting it as a deepest wisdom against the poor women.

Reprinted and translated into German, Dutch, Italian, Spanish, English and Portuguese, it outsold all other books except the Bible!

For the benefit of the reader, that might not be familiar with the content of this now almost forgotten book, without a wish to enter into its cruel and disturbing mental core, just a glimpse of this document will keep zou awake at night.

'All wickedness, is but little to the wickedness of a woman...' is written in the manual. *'What else is woman but a foe to friendship, an inescapable punishment, a necessary evil, a natural temptation, a desirable calamity, domestic danger, a delectable detriment, an evil nature, painted with fair colours... Women are by nature instruments of Satan - they are by nature carnal, a structural defect rooted in the original creation.'*

We share with you this thought left in many, of how can anyone in their right mind allow the book that carried within its pages these sentences, to become readily accessible to uneducated mob, thirsty for scandals, Devil's blood and punishment?

No wonder, the mob was fascinated with the idea of witches, flying monsters devouring kids and having secret sexual allegiances with the Devil.

In the middle of the night, they cuddled their kids even closer, as the nights are scary, the peak time for the transformation, ruling the darkness of starry nights: stealing good health, good fortune, poisoning cattle, and destroying crops.

Fanatics demanded many drops of Eva's blood... A crazy revenge for the paradise lost, sadomasochism that has back-fired, creating a forest fire burning thousands, maybe millions of trees.

Some high officials, read - a very few educated and cultured men, accepted the ways of the hunt and stopped questioning or using their reason if they ever had one.

"For what is written and published must be the highest of truths!" This is why I have never put any of my thoughts to writings. Pythagoras was back.

In the ancient European society the humanity fought so hard to establish the law as the norm, they abandoned all legal procedures and norms, aware that not a single woman would be accused if the procedure was governed by the law.

You must have heard of Parthenon (Ancient Greek: Παρθενών), a temple on the Athenian Acropolis dedicated to the goddess Athena built around 440 BC? Asked Pythagoras

With the most unfortunate history of our religious wars, the ancient Parthenon was first converted into a Christian church in 600 AC and during the Ottoman rule in Greece, from 1453, in to a mosque. Yet it managed to survive until 1687, when the Pope and the Venetian Governors assembled the so-called "Venetian" army, and send a general Morosini to fight the Ottoman Empire. In his unsuccessful siege of the city the Acropolis was bombarded continuously for eight days, and on September 26, 1687, a bomb hit the storage gunpowder magazine and completely blew it apart.

The subconscious material or mind chitta has its own "body" that engulfs the Soul. Each soul from its birth passes through various awakenings, or dissociation from the sub-consciousness. Meditated Pythagoras

Mind chitta is an astral vibratory response within the subconscious layers with the precise words, feelings, and thoughts formations. We all enter it unconsciously. An ancient Indian Philosopher Patanjali recognized these dynamics in his Yoga Sutras. Said the bat.

The infinite divisibility of the atom with its rapid transformation prevents the Soul from manifesting. Two atoms react uniquely different when with each other and two Souls have uniquely different encounters. Two mothers exchange parenting knowledge, two grandpa share their illnesses; two lovers interact through a sexual contact. The circumstances dance within the Universal Flow, creating a type of Dough that subconsciously modifies our thinking principle as a Soul materialized on Earth or someone who belongs to a Group. We naturally belong to various Groups: age, nationality, profession, religion and 90% of our subconscious mind "belongs" to these dynamics making us learn from each other, yet the conscious manipulation or the "moulding" of any group's dynamic is not a recent phenomenon within Human History. Chuckled Pythagoras.

Passing the time portal, a few days ago, both the Heritage Malta and the Serbian Heritage have inaugurated Roman Villas that were occupied for at least six centuries from 200 BC to 400 AC. The villas were olive and wine producing within their little ancient merchandising worlds. In both cases, note, how misleading the name is the "Roman Villa" makes us travel to Rome in our minds, yet the age points to the Eastern Roman Empire where the Byzantine Kingdom of Greece was.

My Ancient Greece was known as Hellas, said Pythagoras, and our ancient maps show it as the centre of the world surrounded by the Mediterranean Sea. Malta, South Italy, Crete, Greece, Ancient Europe, the so disputed area of Thrace and Macedonia, Istanbul (later Constantinople) was also a part of this world full of Islands and coastal cities.

At the corner, where Heaven meets the Earth, two mice had a chaise around a slice of bread.

Come closer. Over here is the precious work of art, a bird's nest left abandoned, from the summer three years ago. Still surviving the test of time.
"Well, I must say the creature is rather charming, leaving the traces of flowers behind its tail, or is it a butterfly in its shade..."

Gaze fixed beyond his shoulder, an English tourist passes by.

"My gratitude, Madam, for your generosity", whispered a man touched by the scene. Sha*woman*ka of an intricate nature flew passed this morning horizon of the astral realm, listening to a baby whining in her dreams. The sparkling realms of sand extended beyond the imaginative into the spheres of Gods.

Archaeologists on their quest, explorers of once real gathered to examine the soil. Enough remains of the building to give an idea of its former grandeur, on the summit of the hill, the ruins of a compound consisting of twelve houses forming a square.

To the North we flew, in search of lost richness, to the South in search of Goodness, to the East towards the rising Sun, to the West to meet the Kings. None knew will we succeed. For it was the Labyrinth we feared, the Labyrinth of Government rules, Religions dogmas, neighbours' set in concrete mind set, towards the Silk Road and the giant cobra expressing the secret of aNX (anch), the secret of the resurrection of the soul from and back into the hands of Holy Spirit. Pythagoras added picking up a stone observing its shape.

Lovers merged to unite with Tao. The inn-keeper never minded the noise for the couple had the same surname, newly wed they said, and that is not against the rules.
Hundreds of faces flocked the market that eve, seeking peace in unruly shopping. Black Friday, if you please, of any hemisphere at any time of our history.

Its face silvered by the moon's shadow, the lake mirrored an approval, or was it a disapproval? He needed the approval in order to define himself - as a ghost or a shadow or a thought form just about to disappear, so let it be, the Luna's reflection said: "I approve of you!"

The church elite and judges,

Who are supposed to protect us...

...started their malicious hunt with an amazing zeal.

No cost too great, no number too high and no logic too inverted to serve the greater good of Christianity.

Yes, you ought to be familiar with this scenario, it is not the first time that a murderer 'saves' not only his soul but the souls of his beloved villagers, killing a wicked Shakti, cleansing the Earth of Evil as the End of the World approached.

End of the World, of course, another nonsense!

Our fellow men, for women were at home nursing numerous children, from all around the planet: Portuguese, Spanish, Germans, Italians, English, and French all believed in the conspiracy of the Devil to destroy the Christian world.

The hunt begun and no mercy was ever shown. The torture and execution became a necessary evil. Sisters, mothers, neighbours, lovers, all, came under the attack of the faithful. Being different, standing out in beauty or sickness, rich or too poor, or unlucky to have a 5 year old dreaming a witches' gathering, the fearful dream was a mighty proof for the inquisitors!

So, children were witnesses? Asked the bat, surprised with the stupidity of human nature.

Oh, yes! Sometimes the main ones! Kids as young as five would be called as witnesses. Their vivid imagination gave the priests and the mob plenty of mind-chitta materials. Madness within the circles of the ruling class, different kastas, the madness of the hunt!

In reality, no 'doing' was crazy to comprehend, for the accusers thoughts of sacrificing new-born babies, or causing natural disasters, droughts, floods and diseases.

A religious war against the worshipers of any faith, quite a handful thought! The bat moved closer to her lover.

A typical craze would start with one or two suspects and through the forced confessions would spread indefinitely. The longer the panic the larger the numbers, and of course wealthier the victims.

Get this, a French witch hunter, Pierre de Lancre, accused, believe it or not, ALL 30,000 inhabitants of Laboured of witchcraft, priests included! He succeeded in executing around 600 women in the region.

A German witch hunt could kill hundreds in a single city, in Würzburg the number was 1200. The Catholic archbishop of Cologne, boasted that he burned 2,000 members of his flock during the 1630s. The witch prosecution spread from Northern Italy to Poland, Germany, France, Switzerland, and England. Our time became the Burning Time.

Can you imagine, your mother or sister within this cycle of nightmares?

Can you imagine all the medical knowledge passed through the centuries and shared amongst wise women, midwives and women healers disappear, burnt during these Burning Times?

Luckily, not all of Europe got the bug. My Spain was protected...

Really, what has happened?

Alonso Salazar, a Spanish inquisitor, a man of notorious reputation for burning heretics in Spain, was the one to stop witch-hunting in his region.

How come? What happened?

Salazar was a judge in a trial that threatened to engulf 1,800 suspects, of which 1,500 were children, in his Navarra region. As a lawyer, his common sense guided him to reject the statements of children. He visited the supposed witches gathering places and interrogated in details the women that gave their testimony, about where the devil sat and how the ceremony looked like.

Of course, they all contradicted each other. He cooked supposed poisons, and ointments, and they all proved to be harmless and fake created by women to satisfy blood thirsty curiosity of their persecutors. In fact, none amongst 2,000 people involved has ever seen a witch. Salazar realised that the Devil hides in unjustly accusing the innocent. He freed all the accused and the Spanish Inquisition never executed another witch.

"I thought that this far, in Macao, we would be free from this madness." After a moment of silence, a shadow under the tree said.

"Ama is a witch! Fra Thomas claimed, but we will see for how long this absurd accusation can hold."

An absurd accusation indeed, but this was the century with absurdity as the middle name of much that has happened. The 16th and 17th century tip-toed over the Earth with the clumsiness of a Giant, shaking the roots of all past beliefs, leaving huge finger prints all throughout scientific work and religious structures.

These centuries saw changes in knowledge, culture, and conscious behaviour; our unconsciousness, habits, and good old superstitions stayed within our make-up for a while longer, lingering there, waiting for some other spiritual revolution to happen hundreds of years later.

This was the time of the first telescope discovery and the time of the earliest really precise star movement observations. The time when mathematicians and astronomers for the first time challenged our homocentric cosmology, and its obsession with the mighty-human-centric quantum reality!

Pythagoras stopped the story in mid-air! But it wasn't always like that! He siad.

Flourishing blossoms of an oRCHaRD and peaches of immortality remind the artists that whenever they pick up their painting brushes, their symbols will shine GOLD. The opening and closing rhythms of the compositions resonate the same way the limestone beneath a mountain's breath. Guided by bare-legged moon-ladies dressed in white, saints of all religions have the intuitive visions of the future, heaven or hell. Pilgrims venturing the mountains' passes hear enchanting melodies of the Ladies of Tao, as a sound of bees or a distant flute.

Let me take you to a different time and place, said Pythagoras, time and space travelling us to Egypt to the Petrie excavation in 1897, of Six Temples at Thebes, during the time known as the New Kingdom, of Ancient Egypt.

We (me as a spirit and the researchers back in time) have approached the city of Amarna from the north by river, the first buildings ran all the way up to the waterfront being the main residence of the Royal Family. The Northern Suburb was initially a prosperous area with large houses, but the house size decreased further from the road. Most of the important buildings were located in the central city and so was the Bureau of Correspondence of Pharaoh, where the Amarna Letters were found. The Bureau of Correspondence! Can you comprehend that!!!

As in the Ancient Egypt or Ancient European Danube Culture, those who worshiped her wished to achieve a new birth in death. Nut, the Egyptian all Mother sky Goddess, arches over Earth to swallow the Sun, to let Ra run through her body during his night journey, so she symbolised the Cosmic power that is all encompassing, all knowing, and enlightening, the great mother that when drawn inside the Ancient Egyptian coffins promised the same nurture and rebirth for the souls of the dead.

Just before we approach the city of Amarna that exists no more but in our imagination, a bird eye view, from Google maps, zooms us in to recently discovered archeological findings of deserted shrines to the West and East Mother goddesses, carved back within caves, in the sides of the mountain ranges of Mount Sha, down in Ancient Egypt and up the sacred path across the waters, across Sinay, to the Ancient Greece and

Balkans, up the Danube river, all through the Islands of Mediterranean, to Cyprus, Crete, Malta, to the South of Italy into Croatia, Serbia, Macedonia, Bulgaria, carved in the rock at the mouth of the caves, worshipping Goddess Moon whilst her long rays caresses the altars.

The tinkling of the water could not mark the passage of time, so no traces are left of the Priestesses sacred fire, initiation times of Tao, virgin births, water rituals of baptism, resurrection after death rituals, so Ank or Anch or AnX, blessed sign of Venus, representing holy spirit sent forth by the Goddess, enters a soul, and returns back to God ending its journey on Earth, after dying.

The city of Amarna is an ancient capital city of a region in Egypt, where a Pharaoh Akhenaten (aXeNaTeN = note a striking similarity with the name AleXaNDeR) and his wife Nefertiti ruled. It covered an area of approximately 12 km; on the west bank of Nile, the land was set aside to provide crops for the city's population. The people that lived in the region and found a few settlements including the famous Babylon, called itself aXeN. The construction of the Temple has started in 1,346 BC, by the AXenaten's son, the King Tutan Khamun (Xa+Moon) who was born in Thebes, the modern LuXoR in Egypt.

The entire city was encircled with a total of 1 + 12 boundary stele engraved with carvings. The stele are cut into the cliffs on both sides of the Nile (10 on the east, and 3 on the west) and record the events of AXetaten (aXeTaTeN) from founding to its fall. The document records the pharaoh's wish to have several temples of the Aten = Athen = aXeN. The lingua franca used during, what is now known as the Late Bronze Age, in the area was Akkadian.

In 1887, a local woman has uncovered a cache of over 300 cuneiform tablets now known as Amarna Letters.

All the frescos at ancient temples speak of the constant drive towards an omnipotent, omnipresent God or Goddess that governs all and is not accessible by words or art works. It is a sound but not a form, a concept but not a meaning.

The religious reforms of AXenaten, in the New Kingdom, were aimed at changing the monotheism towards the Female Goddess aXeNa, the story that was later in history referred to as "Amarna Heresy".

The Mediterranean Islands, like Crete, Malta, the South of Italy, the Mount Olimp (Holy Mountain in Greece), Macedonia, Balkan Countries, Egypt, Ethiopia, at the time, had sophisticated spiritual rituals fully archeologically documented as early as 2,500 BC, and have been since fully incorporated within the Christian Church ritual practices and philosophical concepts.

So, why the eXcalibur of a WaRRioR?

We now need a sword that gives all the power, we devote our lives to find it, but only a chosen few can hold it, like a Holy Grail or Lapis Lazuli, it is a word, frequency, symbol, all of it at the same time. Drawing the number one and eight on the sand, but I'll tell you about them later, the sounds of "X" "Š" "Đ" "DŽ" each hiding a story of a different mystical and occult nature.

The images at the Ancient Egyptian Temple site and Ancient Greek philosophers speak of SuN as the number 1 or Omnipresent and Omnipotent Goddess that as its rays emanates aNXs or Holy Spirits or Sounds or Metaphysical Frequencies of Consciousness that enter the body in its journey through the earth. Accumulating experiences of goodness as the highest goal, while reunited with Divine after the death, symbolically, and astraly becoming Gods.

The One that is Xa emanates 9 rays (aNXs) to the Left and 9 rays (aNXs) to the Right, towards the side where the King is seated and to the other side where the Queen is. The two multiply into many, becoming three, for in their hands are the kids, and there are three (3) of them. One (1) that is not a number, but an entity, becomes two, that is a snake, a Kundalini force, a movement, a merge of Yin and Yang, and than three, a triangle of trinity forces that together symbolically form a DECAD (10) or 3 letters hidden within the Sun (YHW or YHSH or YHX) + 9 + 9 Gods or sounds of Gods and Goddesses, each carrying an energy form for "at the beginning there was a word / logos and the word was with God and the word / Logos was God"

The number one as the origin of all things and the dyad as matter while a triangle is a symbol of Apollo. The four is for four elements, the odd numbers (1,3,5,7,9) are masculine and even numbers (2,4,6,8) are feminine. Chanted the bat her knowledge of this subject matter.

With ten being the "perfect number", Earth being spherical, the globe devided into five climatic zones, continued the bat.

Yes, just before the dark ages of European science, harmonics of the world and order of the universe was our musical symphony. Pythagoras added.

After this time, it took Europe ages to accept zero as a number and a concept. Accepting zero, we finally accepted the possibility of an idea that has no form. For some Monastic Orders the adoption of zero was a device of the Devil. Zero provided a framework for the development of atheism. Zero is associated with nil, non-being, nothingness, emptiness, and with zero defining non-quantitative as non-existent, everything non-quantifiable could now be defined as non-existent - including God.

It was Barbarians worshipping Bog (a Slavic name for God) and saying Jai to Vo (Bull) within the word DjaVo (devil) meaning "Jay Vo". It was Barbarians that have passed the knowledge of Amorites, Babylon, Pythagoras within the same region. It was aXeN, Artemis and DioNisus that was worshiped in this area, just at the time of Christ during the legacy of Babylon, Ancient Greece, Maltese Temples, Ancient China, Cyprus Civilization, or Serbian VinČa that had floor heating in houses 4,000 BC.

Most of you probably remember this story: Once upon these times, carving our future, our ancestors dreamt of a new, better, more exciting Christian kingdom, and they sent ships into the vastness of unknown seas, to find the shortest route to the source of gold, exotic spices, silky-skinned women – India. The Destiny led one of the ships off a well-known course, to touch the shore of what is now known as Brazil. The year was 1492, his name is Columbus and he was granted, by the King Ferdinand II of Spain, to equip three ships and sail out west into the Atlantic, in search for a western route to the Orient. The Great Admiral of the Ocean Sea Verily, verily, (he was called that way) landed in the island of San Salvador, discovering a new continent and with it new tastes, sensations and new thoughts.

Potato and tobacco were brought from America, together with coffee that was brought from Africa, the ritual of smoking and drinking tea and coffee entered our veins. Spices and coffee sneaked into the streets of London and Paris and a first slab of chocolate was on sale in Spain. A completely new set of Gods and Deities marched into our conscious and unconscious sphere, influencing the minds of European philosophers, artists and scientists.

The exploration bug entered our blood, transforming all our maps, our diets and our preferences for clothing. After centuries of isolation, the World looked at us, and we looked at the World, and our eyes finally met, in this glow of self-reflection, doubts and challenges. We needed to share it with others.

During the times of Leonardo Da Vinci, Michelangelo and Raphael, the time of nude, luscious sculptures and paintings in churches, that surprise visitors even today with their bare boobs, and pronounced gluteus maximus, we officially as lunatics, marched into the Age of Reason. Our Universities flourished, manuscripts that were for centuries exclusively passed from one monk to the other, were finally discovered, printed and published, and for the first time distributed, freely or in secret, amongst the geeks thirsty of knowledge.

The transition needed a place where all are equal, where commoners can pay their bill, where all can sit together, where one must wait to be served, hence one can listen and talk. This time of transition needed a coffee house.

The preparation of coffee is somewhat complicated, the beans need to be roasted, ground and brewed, so it takes time to serve a customer, there is always plenty of time to 'kill', yet the black liquid is cheap and affordable to all. The coffee houses near the Great Mosque in Cairo and the ones along the waterfront in Istanbul, the simple coffee shops in villages near markets in Yemen, or the big spacious elevated halls in the cities of Persia, the ones in London, Paris and Milan, all had the same in-common, they were visited by scholars, teachers, and students, sitting either on the floor or low benches talking, reading and discussing various manuscripts.

Coffee shops offered all of this: an informal seating that encouraged mingling, a door open to all that can pay a penny for the magic liquid, and a great atmosphere for study, debate and story-telling. They provided a place where different classes could meet and talk more freely than anywhere else, so much so, that in England they got nick named: 'penny universities'.

Coming back to the heart of the Asian continent, now in the 16th and 17th century, Chinese believed that within their Great Walls spreads all true civilisation. Outside it is wilderness and chaos haunted by robbers and barbarians. Within it, there is China, with large and well lit cities with water and drainage, Universities and large libraries, paper money that allows the flow of commerce and growth of trade, markets and industry.

If you didn't know, the Chinese were the ones to invent the press, gunpowder, and the magnetic compass some centuries before these miracle war-inducing goods came to Europe. The land of silk, spices, stunning cities and amazing culture was in those days ruled in order and harmony by their Emperor, Thiencu, the Son of Heaven.

China was these days also governed by some very educated men. It had two special orders of chosen philosophers, whose titles carried a great respect and authority. These wise men task was to advise the King of any violation of the law in any part of the Kingdom and not even the King himself was spared from their scrutiny, and their dishonesty.

The size of their navy at the time is impressive; at the beginning of 15th century they counted more than 1,300 combat vessels, the world's largest and most technologically refined merchant marine and navy. Its ships sailed to the coasts of Africa and back but whilst the nations of Europe seemed to be entirely obsessed with the idea of domination, no Chinese King thought of waging a war against Europe or Africa. For thousands of years tthey used the trade to communicate, crossing the dangerous mountains and hostile deserts, along the Silk Road, transporting and trading precious stones, spices and silk.

After the discovery of the sea route to India, the Portuguese were one of the first to open the trade with all the distant kingdoms of the Far East. They landed and settled for the first time in Macao's small harbour in mid-16th Century.

This is where Ama was born.

Macao started her life as a shelter to weather storms, a port for refugees, mainly missionaries fleeing trouble in other parts of Asia, but was a good choice for settlement because of its perfect position: some 40 miles to the east-northeast, across the mouth of the Pearl River, is Hong Kong, and not further than 100 miles is Canton.

Not long after the first Portuguese built their settlement, Macao developed into a major port for trade and the centre of culture and religion exchange funded by its soon-established virtual monopoly on trade between China and Japan, and Europe and East Asia.

From 1573, collecting phenomenal amounts of gold, and silk and spices, claiming their God's supremacy with guns, bribes, and piracy, following the example of all the major colonising forces throughout the Earth at the time, they demanded autonomy, they established their own governing body with a Governor appointed from Portugal or elected by local Portuguese.

In 1582, disapproving of the Portuguese violation of Chinese governance, the Chinese Main Governor summoned the Governor of Macao, and tried to teach him the rules of law and order, a simple property game we all find familiar today, yet so far from the consciousness of European war and gold thirsty semi-Gods of the time.

The struggle for political supremacy between the two continued for centuries to come.

However, underneath the layers of greed, beneath the selfishness of Royal Courts and Churches, something more mysterious and profound connected the two lands: the Chinese and Europeans.

Stronger than the urge to trade, wage wars, posses, convert, amidst these turbulences, was our fascination with one another, our deep respect for the hidden beauty radiating from the other.

The Chinese Philosophy developed in a different direction than the European one.

Nobody in China thought of studying Nature in an independent, methodical way, they approached it with a sacred awe for the mysteries of Universe, and built an amazing system of beliefs based on ancient mystic formulas, the system deeply rooted in the minds of people, interwoven into their way of life. For the Chinese, Nature is a living organism and its breath lives in everything, producing different conditions of heaven and earth, called: Yang and Yin. The heavens, Yang, give light, warmth and life; while Yin or Terrestrial Breath, brings death and darkness. With the knowledge of the two, one can live happiness, abundance, and peace on Earth.

The wisdom radiating from the ancient Chinese philosophies, wanted to move into the grounds of Europe that desperately needed this 'female' approach to Earth and its beings. Europe that has already experienced it two and more thousand years ago.

Holy water and the sacred word that is all you need. Said a gypsy witch with a snake around her neck.

Maria's tears they are, from the grave of Jesus. Not an item easy to be found. Not a request easy to be settled. A magic key of everlasting happiness...

I'll get you the bottle of tears but for the words, you got to speak with a wizard, a male, from Egyptian gypsies, a Bedouin from the desert, the worshipper of Nuit. Or to an Arab sailor with own boat, a Sufi follower, or to a wondering barefoot priest from Syria, a hermit from the Sinai mountain, Sha Ra where MoShe saw the burning bush. That is a bit more difficult for they talk not to women.

A butterfly flew passed breaking the silence building nets of wisdom somewhere in the space. It whispered...

The philosophical research concerning the divine poses the question: Is there a meaning / sense / purpose to voicing / writing / reading as us finite beings talk about God and Infinity?

Is a human being really able to discuss God and Cosmos?

Knowing God is a mystical experience, first and foremost a subconscious one we wish to go far back in time, because at the time when none travelled, none spoke other languages, and the Humanity was a handfull of human beings, if a civilization within their Lands had an Alphabet, they must have nourished Science as the Supreme Act, so they had art, sports, culture, and researchers that spent their lives exploring.

There is an ethical importance in speaking about God / Goodness / Law totally unconnected to the question of faith, or occult knowing of Tao's existence or non-existence, and whether a Man (as a King or a Fisherman) has the capability to answer this question. Both the ancient Egyptians and Incas remind us that the mystical name of the Sun-Moon God is Amon Ra. Ra or Da as the sounds of the supreme male quality, and Ma or Na as the sounds of the supreme female quality, these two also combining within the name of the Hindu's supreme God B-Ra-Ma, or Be Ra & Ma or within the Christian worlds through the devotion to Marija as Ma + Ra to me (Ya = I)

The Christians have preserved the secret sacred sound of the supreme Egyptian Goddess, aXeN praying to the name of Xristos. The Arabs will praise AllaH, and the Hindus priests when devoting their prayers to their Supreme Male God will sing: Om Namah SivaYa. The Mystical Tibetan Buddhists use "Aum Mani Padme Hum"

Traveling to the birth place of the western religious movements, we meet the Jewish EloHim: the all-powerful one creator, Elyon: The God Most High, El Roi: The God Who Sees Me, El Olam: The Eternal God, El being the strong one or a universal "La" that is "singing to", "praising".

Of course, we bow to Jehovah: the Lord, or Adonai: the Great Lord, YHWH: as "I AM" or YAH: "I AM H", IMMANUEL: the Supreme God (during the meditation visualizing Cosmos) within us "I AM" IT or the Hindu So HaM.

For decades, the scholars agreed that Jesus most likely grew up in his home at Nazareth, using Aramaic as his mother tongue. Some speculate that Hebrew was only the language of Rabbis, a dead language after the Babylonian Exile. The fact that the Gospels were originally written in Greek show it was widespread in Jesus' time so when he conversed with "Romans" they would have used Greek. Judging the crowds attending the gathering, the scholars concluded that Jesus spoke the entire Sermon on the Mount in Greek.

Now, just listen to the Ancient Greek philosophers' definitions, we are actually speaking of wording used 2,500 years ago!!!

"This logos holds always but humans always prove unable to ever understand it, both before hearing it and when they have first heard it. For though all things come to be in accordance with this logos, humans are like the inexperienced when they experience such words and deeds as I set out, distinguishing each in accordance with its nature and saying how it is. But other people fail to notice what they do when awake, just as they forget what they do while asleep." - Heraclitus (535 – 475 BC).

Philo of Alexandria (20 BC - 50 AC), used the term Logos to mean an intermediary divine being or demiurge. Plato's Theory of Forms was located within the Logos, but the Logos acted on behalf of God in the physical world.

The concept of Logos, in Sufism, is used to relate Divine to mankind, for no contact between man and God can be possible without the Logos.

Plotinus in interpreting Logos as the principle of meditation, gives methods to achieve ecstasy, using Logos, as the Divine Eternal Principle, existing as the interrelationship between the Soul, the Spirit, and the One. For Plotinus, the relationship between the three, by the outpouring of Logos from the higher principle to the Soul, or by Eros (loving) coming from the lower principle. Centuries later, Carl Jung contrasted logos vs Eros represented as the alchemical Sol and Luna, science and mysticism, or conscious and unconscious.

Gods or goodness or law is within the words AMR, in Ancient Egypt translated as the God Amon Ra, in Latin translated as AMORE. Pre Latinization, pre Supreme Male God Philosophy entered our minds, souls and lives, the one that was given to us by our wise ancestors as

MaRRy, the sacred name for LOVE. The one that has put forward the first command "Do not Kill" in an attempt to safeguard the Humanity's efforts to reach God / Goodness / Divine.

There are 21 discovered symbols / stamps within Ancient Serbian Vinča culture that dates back to 6000 BC. Can this be a coincidence? Through the trade, the Ancient Chinese have passed the numbers 1-10 as sacred symbols, within the philosophical set-up of Taoism as: Yin and Yang, a male and female representation of Cosmos, that within its forces manifest as 10 symbols x 2 = 20 + 1 that is Tao (Yin and Yang combined) the same as the one found in Egyptian / Phoenician alphabet, or Jewish Kabbalah, that within its wisdom talk about God, creation, divine, Tao, Female and Male consciousness manifestation forces, Kundalini awakening with its journey back to Goddess.

The two were meant to merge and Macao became the symbol of this merge, an alchemical egg that has morphed into a mythical beast of the times yet to come.

Macao's Goddess that protects the little peninsula and supports her growth is A-Ma. People of Macao believed in A-Ma, and fishing boat returning to the harbour took turns to line up in front of the temple giving A-Ma their offerings.

As it is with all magical stories, Macao or the Bay of A-Ma, is symbolically connected to the mainland by a sand land bridge, creating a peninsula in the shape of a lotus flower.

Various stories and miraculous rescues of the fisherman caught in the rough sea were connected to the Goddess A-Ma. The most famous is the story of a girl who dreamt of her father and brothers caught in a storm and who tried to help them in her dream. Her mother was alarmed with the uneasiness of her child's sleep and she shook her to wake her up, causing her, in her dream, to let go of one of the boats. Later, the story goes, her brothers returned without their father, recalling a terrible storm and the vision of a beautiful girl, their sister, coming to save them but vanishing just before she was able to hold onto their father's boat that disappeared within the roughness of the sea. The girl, appearing as a spirit, continued helping boats in trouble bringing the sailors to safety for many centuries.

Another tale is the one of a fisherman boat giving a free passage to a peasant girl and being saved from a typhoon that destroyed all the other larger vessels. When the small boat landed in Macao, the girl walked to the shore and mysteriously disappeared in a glow of light. The passenger of the boat was none other than Goddess herself.

The fishermen built a temple in her honour at the entrance of Macao's inner harbour.

The legend that most profoundly relates to the deeper levels of our story is the one of the Sun Goddess Ama-Theresu.

Once upon a time, Sun Goddess, Ama-Theresu, had a horrible fight with her brother, Storm God, and after one of those tiresome, scary arguments only a brother could contemplate and with the full scrutiny execute, she got so hurt that for a moment of insanity she forgot her real Nature and decided to escape and retreat into a cave. She blocked the entrance of her new abode with a large stone, leaving the rest of the world in Darkness.

Oh, mighty heavy was the Darkness! A minute after minute, an hour after hour, a night after night, all the living creatures that depend on Her Light waited for Her return. Long is the wait that is filled with fear, grave is the thought of even a possibility of the Goddesses disappearance. To no avail were tears of lilies and butterflies, that have shorter lives and for it even deeper connection to Her Light, the Sun was not to be seen in the skies, She was hidden in her dark abode and nobody could entice her out. The Lady Balance that rained on Earth before this moment, hid Her face within the lava of a newly born volcano, allowing Chaos to prevail winning its game of Death and Destruction, Life as we know it, started to wane.

After the 4th night, even Gods got worried. Their words were useless against Her fears, and they realised that they had to bring Her back to the purpose of Her own existence.

An Oracle was called to shine the Light into this little game of unconsciousness, to gather the energies of the Beginning and the End, and give a hint of where the Key to this puzzle hides.

Create an atmosphere of Magic and Wonder in front of Her cave, the Oracle said, the atmosphere that triggers curiosity even of the tinniest forest spirits, the energy of game, excitement, trill, that might entice Her Majesty to look outside. Chose a woman that will dance her way into infinity, eternity, Golden Light, using Maya of different realities.

Nothing less than the purity of Her own Being will make the Goddess return to the Path of Life. She has to be exposed to Her own Light, the Oracle said.

Hang up a mirror at the entrance of Her cave, Oracle was revealing the clever plot. Entice Her to look outside.

And who is the maiden? Gods looked around.

And the Oracle said: You will find Her amongst the Stars. She has many names.

Nuit is one of Her names, Holder of Stars. She carries a lantern oiled with innocence and joy, her voice is a soothing melody and her touch is one of an angel. If she finds you wondering in the middle of a tunnel of shadows, lost, fighting against own and other people's devils, living within self-created nightmares, She will take you by the hand and deliver you to the World of Colours.

Alchemy is Her name, a witch, a doctor, a magician, an artist of transformation, a principal force that leads a

Soul's journey to its Merge with the Holy Spirit. Unpredictable, she experiments playing with Gods and Devils. She guides the union manipulating energies to accelerate our transformation.

She is Maria, Virgin Mother, a protector that is always awake. The Embodiment of Strength and Wisdom that is capable of carrying pain of generations to come. She understands and forgives fully, unconditionally, and patiently turns back to Love.

She is Kali, a Principal Force of Destruction, a carrier of storms, a fierce Goddess that brings fear to humanity, incarnating terror. With skeletons around her neck, and corpses as her carpet, she dances, screaming, demanding from her followers a complete renunciation. She shrieks that the ultimate nature of Life is Death. Laughing at our pain, sending it back, over and over again, until we learnt our lessons, she is a dark and ugly, evil manifestation of Self.

Her name, said the Oracle, will this time be Ama, a female that sleeps in every one of us, Yin of Creation, a wisdom guide that with her purity extinguishes thirst for spiritual longings. She is the one that stands on a crescent moon with stars in her hair, pouring water from jars of her soul into lakes of emotions, awakening compassion for humankind and its Chaos, nourishing Earth and Her constant renewal.

Materialised in a female body, through centuries, with the life of an ordinary person, She ascends to meet the ones that are ready for Her, that call Her, that have a wish to understand. She is the personification of the Universal Mother. She lives Love and Clarity and She dies at Will, when She decides that it is time to go.

Her name is Ama.

There was an Ama in the village, a girl at a peak of her vitality that had 'abundance' written on her forehead, just emerging from the search for identity, growing into a wonderful human being. As a fragile essence rising from the foam of a rough sea, she was gentle and giving in her openness, powerful and overwhelming in her beauty.

Gods called Ama and told her of a plan to organize a huge gathering in front of the Goddess's cave asking her to dance for them. Ama was to give a performance that would remove obstacles from the hearts of man, hoping that the noise of Happiness, Delight and Joy will intrigue Sun Goddess to come out from her hiding place.

Ama was a beautiful young dancer that enchanted many in a nearby village and had a body and a zeal of a Goddess. Ama knew that her dance is going against all the odds of depression and distress. She knew that the hope was gone from the minds of Man. Looking at the sky, night after night, in vain, waiting for Her arrival and observing everything sink into Darkness had scared and tired them. She felt her task was difficult. She needed to create an illusion of Light that would lead to the release of pure Light.

The gathered crowd was waiting, grumbling, gossiping, and whispering. None and all felt like partying, none and all understood why they were there. In the middle of their anxiety music brought by stars and Ama emerged, dancing her Magic, encircled with Beauty that is Pleasure and Bliss.

Carried by the Divine Ecstasy she drummed using her feet and hands, her voice became an instrument, she swayed in the rhythm of breathing, using her knowledge of non-breathing, she carried Life on her naked shoulders. Awakening spirits, enchanting Gods, and rejoicing people was the core of her dance that instantly healed the doomed, sick and tired minds.

Torches uncovered colours of her flesh, glow of her smooth skin became an invitation to her Dance. She had nothing to lose and everything to gain: the salvation of all living beings on Earth. With her dance her body became a prayer wheel connecting Life and Death, creating Timelessness within the Space of this Myth.

Her beauty unfolded shining the energy of Creation.

Dancing with Gods, people and animals, teasing them with her nakedness, her burning body was moving effortlessly through the crowds inviting them to forget their troubles and join this crazy festivity.

The invitation came too sudden to refuse, too strong not to be noticed and crowds started moving and clapping, feet followed the rhythm and within minutes the air was filled with laughter of approval, hooting and shouting; Man lit thousands of torches forgetting their misfortunes, Gods joined in the celebration; animals and cocks began crowing loudly in unity, and it felt as though Earth for a moment regained its Balance: the ecstasy and delight returned. The Essence became Now, past and future disappeared.

And yes, the plot has worked!!! Sun Goddess was surprised to hear all the noise of happiness outside Her cave. World was supposed to be dying in Darkness without Her! Moving the stone to see what caused all the cheer the Sun Goddess caught a glimpse of Her own reflection in the mirror hanging in front of the cave and got transfixed by the image, by Pure Light. This sight has reminded Her of who She really was and at once destroyed Darkness hidden in Her heart making Her return to the reserved palace in Heavens and vow never again to be frightened by any storm and never again to hide from the sight of Gods, men, or Earth.

The beautiful naked girl was standing amidst the delighted crowd that was enchanted by the sight of Sun's return. Ama, with her purity and determination, managed to win the world of shadows, fears, and death that succeeded in seducing even Sun Goddess herself.

Ama, of our story, was born inside this temple at noon of 21st of June 1593, by an African mother, a wife of a Portuguese Lord, Ottavio de Nobille.

Gold is the first and the most perfect of the elements. Gold comes from the centre of the earth, and while it passes through warm and pure places, it becomes the subtlest and purest element on Earth.

It is the most beautiful of all metals, the best that Nature can produce and no other element can corrupt it, or change it.

For what the eagle is among birds, the lion among beasts, the Sun among planets, such gold is among metals. The legend says that the centre of the sun emanates gold, by its rays to all beings. It is a life substance that penetrates all living things.

And all the beings on Earth carry within a grain of gold, hidden deep within their inmost centre - a precious grain of gold. Our core is golden, and when our body gets perfected and our mind gets purified, when we cleanse the uncleanness from it, we will reach within the centre of our beings, our own most precious gold.

Ruben

Her skin, dark olive, tight and silky, her eyes, shape of almonds, piercing and deep, her hands, carved iron, fingers long, jet-black curly hair, and a gracious swan-like neck. Even though I wouldn't admit it, at the time, I wanted her from the very moment I saw her.

I got to know Ama during the Dutch attack on Macao, the 24th of June 1622.

The future generations will also remember the 24th June, 1622, they will call it the 'Dia da Cidade' or the City Day, the day of miracles, the day of a fight with the Dutch, who also had their eyes on our fast-growing trade centre, that was now virtually controlling the European - Far East trade route. During the last couple of years, Macao became the target of repeated invasion attempts, culminating with this most violent and dangerous one in June 1622.

Macao is hot and damp in summer, especially when there are no winds coming from the ocean or interludes of typhoon. Once or twice a year, the humidity reaches its highest point, the hot air swells over the Land and it becomes impossible to move or breathe or work, the settlement gets lulled into its yearly sleep. Once or twice a year, the heat becomes unbearable, it becomes the master, it spreads over the stone narrow streets covering us with dust and sticky sweat, and both, animals and people fight against this sickness of Earth, locked within their shelters. At the time of the attack Macao was asleep.

At around noon a fisherman came back to the city alarmed with the sight of a fleet of Dutch galleons. He entered the church breathless, almost crying, grasping for air, panicking, and told me, the local Jesuit Portuguese priest, the man left in charge:

that this was our last day

that there was no hope for our Land

that there was no God that can help us

that there was no worst nightmare than this that was just approaching us.

The moment when 13 huge ships appeared on the horizon manned by thousands of men was a moment of Hell for the citizens of these 3 small islands.

Macao gathered traders from Portugal and Spain, it gathered survivors of shipwrecks, refugees that managed to escape Dutch prisoners' ships and others who found mercy from pirates escaping cruel death. The population in 1622 was already an amazing mix of Portuguese, Asians and Africans.

Today, when the priests and the city council did their fast estimate of people able to fight they added up only 600 men aged over 12, and almost 3,000 women and children older than 8 with around 500 African slaves. Macao has much more inhabitants but this was a very good time for trade and the army of men was miles away in inland China trading their porcelain, silk and spices. We were really just a handful, compared to the thousands of soldiers that were about to embark on the island.

God why did you forsake us? – were the words that roamed my mind for what felt like an hour after I heard that Dutch were going to attack.

Everything was against us: the humidity of this summer day, the settlement deeply affected by the heat and the lack of air, the fortress, Monte Fort that was far from its completion, and the atmosphere of the crowd in front of the church, the atmosphere of fear, despair and anger towards God that sends this type of challenge.

The ships surrounded us and they looked mighty and evil. The so long dreaded attack of Dutch was finally there, about to happen. One is never ever really ready for death.

My mind was in shambles.

Destiny would have it that I started my journey to China with a close encounter with Death. During the night of my ship-wreck, even though I trusted the skills of our Captain and the strength of the ship that was our home all the way from Portugal, the storm that we had encountered was so strong that it shook all my confidence and awakened all my fears.

When it started, it raged for hours increasing its strength and fury with every moment that passed. The rain came down in torrents and during this wrath, we never once saw the sun by day, nor the stars by night. The tempest was so fierce that no one could remain on his feet. The noise was so deafening that we could not hear even our own voices. My fear was so thick that I thought my head is going to burst when the ship gave its first terrible threatening jerk. If I remember correctly, it was the 3rd day of our nightmares, when we hit a rock just off the Formosan coast where the ship gave up its fight delivering us to the sea. The woodland under our feet cracked and disappeared and I was not sure what was spreading faster, water or panic overcoming the crew. The creaks coming from the hull convinced me that we are now at God's Grace and that only He could save us from the ill fate of disappearing within the depths of the glum waters. For the first time I became fully aware of Her Majesty - Death.

All through the days of ship-wreck, Death was steadily breathing down my neck. What an ugly and powerful face she had!

This little episode had a happy ending, once we managed to build our little improvised boat, we set off for a new adventure expecting the worst, but after some days of calm sailing and a calm sea, God's giving, we reached the cost of Macao with almost three hundred survivors.

At this point of our little story, a small transgression, before I tell you all about our little war-tale with the Dutch, I feel an urge to introduce myself, give you a brief sketch of my background, my hopes and thoughts at this stage of life.

I entered the Jesuits in Rome at the beginning of this century when I was 17 and I was ordained a Jesuit three years later taking a special obedience to the Pope undertaking to go wherever I am sent. My Love for Jesus, Truths of Religion, and the quest for Self-Knowledge led me to choose this path, the path that demanded extreme Faith, extreme Sacrifice and extreme Hardship, the path of a Spiritual Warrior. Like all the others, I took the vow of poverty, and the vow of refusal of external honours, material worlds did not interest me.

Going to foreign lands, being surrounded by unfaithful, by dangerous customs, diseases, strange people, was inevitable, but I had nothing to lose spreading Jesus's teachings and delivering more souls to salvation.

Deeds, not words, interested me, dwelling in the Holy Land imitating the life of Christ, or becoming a missionary, devoting my whole life to bringing Christianity to the East was my mission.

After I received permission from my superiors, I embarked on a Portuguese merchant ship with the greatest zest heading to China.

The Dutch fleet started its approach at the same time when I started panicking:

We had just a dozen of cannons and an unfinished Fort

and a bunch of kids, women and slaves.

Nothing more than a dozen of cannons!
God why did you forsake us? I couldn't help thinking!

Like an animal trapped in a cage, pacing up and down, thinking the same useless thoughts, not seeing a way out, not knowing how to re-collect, not understanding, I tried to appear calm.

God why did you forsake us? Was the scream that kept bouncing of the walls of my cell.

All I heard was Silence, a God mighty Silence. My mind was too upset to hear signs from Heaven.

The Fort built by us, Jesuits priests and locals, some years ago, was looking at us. This mix of mud, shells and straw, was our only hope. The mixture packed into place could, perhaps, withstand a hail of cannonballs.

But for how long?
      And why?
           How long before the defeat?
Are we heading towards suicide?

What were our choices?

The stories of horrors roamed in my head, executions and isolation, torture and merciless killings...

Was that God tempting my Faith?

I screamed my question in the silence of my room.

She appeared from nowhere wearing her colourful sarong.

We have no time to waste! she said

      There is no other choice.

           Let's find the shelter within Monte Fort.

A beautiful African youth with the name of the Goddess who it was rumoured knew how to speak with ghosts and animals. The ones who admired her talked about her as of a guide, the scared ones were unnaturally polite to her. She was loved and hated by many.

Her unusual background, her figure, voice, manners, all of her, just couldn't pass unnoticed. If she was born in any other Christian country she would have been marked as a saint or burnt as a witch, but in Macao, she was a walking legend.

A daughter of an African mother she walked gracefully, gliding through our mortals' worlds as though she was just a passer-by observing our struggle to survive untouched by our pettiness, and trivialities, always within her supreme state of peace.

Ama lived in the house of her father, Ottavio de Nobille and she was his favourite. The fairy-tale woven around Ottavio de Nobille, his wife and his daughter Ama, during the long, cold winter evenings, among fishermen and lay-people, were many. The gossips whisper about ancestors' ghosts and angels, and sometimes even Goddess Herself intervening in this child's birth and life, they talk about unspeakable love that existed between Ottavio and his wife and about her magic death.

Ottavio de Nobille came to Macao around 30 years ago bringing with him his wealth, vast knowledge, his laboratory, and books about Philosophy, Astronomy, Art, Natural Sciences, and a spectrum of secrets about the reasons for his immigration to Asia.

Ama's mother got violently sick while giving birth the very day they landed to Macao, and the crew brought her to shore, into the Ama's temple soon after the first contractions have started. The baby girl was born healthy but unfortunately nobody was able to save her mother. One life was sacrificed for the other, the legend narrates, and to thank the Goddess for saving his child, Ottavio gave her the name of A-Ma – the Great Mother.

The day, when 13 Dutch ships appeared on the horizon surrounding Macao, only a miracle could save us and I felt within the depth of my being that Ama was to create that miracle.

Faced with the danger, my mind was divided into two, three, five different personalities and speculatively worked against me, wasting my powers and precious time.
I can!

I can't!
    You can't!
But they might attack the village core killing all the kids!
    We can defend if we retreat!
        The men are out travelling!
But they will soon know our numbers...
    It is useless, if we surrender they might be open to negotiation!

My many 'I's all screamed at the same time, fighting, whispering, moving within me, bringing clouds of weaknesses, dragging deeper into the abyss of my own fearful imagination.

If you have ever experienced a close embrace with the force of fear, its dark and cold touch, its sweaty smell and with the never ending spiral downwards into its core, with every breath my hope was gone, confidence diminished, my core soaked with the icy power that paralyses all the movements.

Citizens of Macao were in panic repeating my own thoughts, yet expecting my guideline searching for the guidelines from Heavens.

"They are on the way!"
    "The ships are approaching"
        "If only our men were here"

"We have the Forth, we must retreat" This was a female voice, an inspiring voice, shiny eyes, a head held high, she was passing Her inspiration through me, thank God I have recognized her, I woke up and started moving.

Fear and despair turned the force of their direction.

It is hard to explain how this has happened. What an invisible force guides us? Angels perhaps? Archangels? In a few moments, moments that lasted an eternity, the impossible became our Reality and Death was not a Threat any more.

Retreating to Monte Fort, high on the hill in the centre of Macao.

A puppet of a Miracle orchestrated on the hill tops of Olympus, I was. Transformed into Moses' magic stick, opening waters for Jewish refugees passing through.

That day, during the fight against the Dutch, I followed the intuitive voice that trusted Ama, and I took the role of the guided and the guide.

Everybody including slaves, women and children were with me, ready to die and ready to follow.

From time to time, in my quest for further guidelines, I would turn to find her facing Chinese, Africans and Portuguese encouraging them with the same determination, just changing the tongues of her speech.

This was my first battle ever. I feared this was Her first battle too. With minimal chances our sword was bravery, our shield - complete trust. Intuitively she was my perfect general and I was her perfect warrior. With no time for doubt with actions coming from divine we let ourselves be led.

The Dutch were about to disembark and the war game was about to begin.

From the Fort we could see clearly:

"Galleons are landing and tens of boats leaving the ships", I've heard her say, observing the mighty army rowing towards Macao.

We knew that they were many, they did not know our numbers. We lost our fear, their fear was on our side. We lost our minds, their thoughts and doubts were inspiring us.

Admiring Ama's determination to fight for lives of Macao's women and children, the army approaching us must have the same mighty impression I had with my first encounter with Macao's Goddess A-Ma.

The temple devoted to A-Ma was the first building I saw when I have for the first time landed in this little settlement.

The temple built by fishermen is on the cliff facing the sea, and it appears from nowhere smiling at the newcomers. Flying eaves and carved lions looked at me from above, reflecting the light of the dawn, receiving me with the grace and superiority. Magical and mystical and yet so real, this architectural miracle stood in its simple perfection manifesting Heavens on Earth. After months of travelling, and the fatigue of our encounter with Death, it was not easy to resist this sight, my heart was filled with a unique mixture of respect and obedience.

The maze of red-hued prayer halls, pavilions and altars, Gods and Goddesses that ruled these lands, for an instant of amazement and insanity, opened a worshiping paradise within my heart. Centuries of prayers instilled the energy of harmony and purpose into the walls of this temple. When I have first arrived, I fell on my knees and kissed the earth: A-Ma was calling me...

Today I knew, there is no soul that could stay untouched by this sight. From the villagers' point of view the smell of offerings: flowers, fruits, and candles, and the sense of complete devotion that this place carried within its walls is enchanted...

Yet from the new-comers point of view, the network of climbing gardens surrounding the temple, the shapes, the magic of this fabled place, the mysticism could have only brought fear.

The ancestor worship and life with the spirits, the superstition and supernatural, became the essence of this encounter. Today, when Death was just minutes away from us, I saw African slaves calling their spirits and living-dead, Chinese pleading to their ancestors and different Gods for help, Christians and non-Christians praying together, people of different religions united against a common enemy, lighting candles as one, and this scene changed something essential within me. A crack of an enlightened idea of a possibility of non-Christian, non-Buddhist, non-pagan, not-named God carved its path amongst neurons of my brain waiting for its moment to break the stone of firmly set beliefs that I called mine for many decades.

While converting Chinese into Christianity to replace worship of idols, I would give my converts images of the cross to adore and teach them to light candles on the altar in admiration of Christ and Holy Marry. Today, candles were the same, they were lit to all Gods – to Christ, to A-Ma, and to Buddha - showing our respect to all, burning for Life.

Looking Death in the eyes, with the Force behind Creation supporting us, we were united in the fight to save our lives.

Children and women into groups of seven, all around the fort, chanting war sounds following rhythms of cannons' fire, giving the impression of multitude of fearsome warriors. Soon, shouting and sounds of horns were coming from everywhere within the fortress.

The strength was on their side, the illusion of strength on ours. Our battle could not last long, time was not on our side, we had to act fast. We could not afford face-to-face combat, we could not afford them knowing our numbers. We were loud and united in our despair.

The cannons in our hands, none knew how to shoot but we were striking in unity. Some of the firemen were children, just passed the adolescence age, and they were most amazed by what a gun could do. Perhaps they were all waiting for this moment of bravery that each boy eagerly looks for and each mother silently resents, listening to the stories of grown-ups around the fire, just after the dinner, the stories mostly invented to be scarier and more exciting than the reality. We had no protection of guards and soldiers, of trained muscles and strong army, the only protection we could hope for was the protection from Above.

We aimed and observed. Every time we hit the target we screamed celebrating our temporary victory. We aimed and shouted. The Fort was on fire, our euphoria was at its pick.

A lucky shot (if such a thing as 'luck' exists) from a cannon on the walls of Monte Fort hit the Dutch gunpowder boat resting in the bay and created a huge explosion that caused attackers to panic. We saw smoke and heard screams, the Chaos was in their lines. This gave us further strength, God was on our side. We had nothing to lose, lives we have already left behind.

In the mist of smoke and heat of our exited bodies I heard chanting in the background, candles lit everywhere, lost in the smoke and purity of our beliefs. We have surrendered and this surrender made us Whole.

Music was getting louder and the beat was encouraging us to move, up front, united, violent, coming from the core of Force unknown to any of us our little army was rapidly spreading disorder through the Dutch in front of us. Another lucky shot and the second ship was on fire and with this one, believe it or not, we managed to injure the Dutch commander.

Noise, smoke, chaos...
    Screams...
        Minutes passing as seconds...

The battle that was decided before it has started...

The outcome defied anybody's belief, the minuscule army managed to sink a few more vessels and in the ensuing confusion we turned into attackers routing the Dutch completely.

The fear was transformed into bravery and almost certain defeat into a victory and our sleepy and scared city became the city of strength, violence and euphoric joy.

Later part of that joy, part of that euphoria, feeling powerful. feeling changed, I wanted to celebrate so I searched for Ama in the crowds and saw her standing peacefully outside the centre of celebrations, steaming with life, glowing within clouds of dust with an expression of somebody whose mission was not yet complete. It was not happiness but stillness that mirrored on her face. Or was it sadness?

"I promise you one thing! I will teach all our children to hate wars!" she said to my surprise.

"There are no winners in a war, there is death and destruction and this barbaric force should not be a part of any human experience." she shared her thoughts weith me some days later.

"On a cosmic scale, a winner will anyhow become a loser and a loser will experience a role of the winner, so why such an urge to kill or hurt, when we are just puppets in this theatre of Life. Within our little journey there is a commandment we still are not ready to hear: DO NOT KILL... DO NOT KILL... DO NOT KILL..."

"So, when we are at the very top, surrounded with the smell of success, we must carefully look at the defeated, at the fellow being that is in trouble."

Ama was among the ones who stayed on the battlefield tending wounded, both the Dutch and the citizens of Macao.

Later that week, Ama and her father, managed to convince the City Council to grant the freedom to all the slaves that were in Macao during the attack, in recognition of their almost suicidal loyalty.

That day I've decided to get to know Ama better.

> For a man to do all that is demanded of him, he must regard himself as greater than he is.
>
> **Goethe**

Father Benedict's Round Table of Solomon

"Every-body and every-thing on Earth lives under the influences of Yin and Yang." said a Chinese man looking deeply serious.

"Every single rock or plant or a water source hides within it a mixture of these two properties, spirits, manifestations and for Life to manifest in its fullest potential, their proportions must be right. Isn't that just fascinating as a theory that if there is too much heat or too much cold the earth will not be fertile, diseases will prevail and people will not live in harmony? Yin follows Yang as birth is followed by death and night by day, joy does not exist without sorrow, nor health without sickness."

Meditating the meaning of Life and Human Existence with my Chinese friends was my favorite past-time.

Sitting inside Ole (Ama and Ottavio's) coffee and tea house we had much to share.

The inside of Ole is quite appealing. It is a simply decorated single large room with cushioned benches running all around the walls. Its simplicity is charming and the whiteness of the walls dances with the outbursts of colours of red and golden silk cushioning. It has a water basin in the middle that gave us all a feeling of peace and tranquillity.

I spent many nights in summer, and days in winter frequenting this place, meeting friends and strangers, reading, writing and discussing both weather and the purpose of life on Earth. I spoke to peasants, craftsman, merchants, slaves, mandarins, all passing through Ole, all classes coming from China, Siam, Malaysia, Ceylon, India, Japan, Philippines, Korea, and all of its frequent customers that returned to its allure year after year for inspiration.

Both, traders and passers-by intermingling on our little peninsula, would find our little hiding place, leaving a bit of themselves every time they came to visit Ole. Macao had regular trade routes to Japan, the Philippines, and Indo China. Exchanging Chinese porcelain, silk, musk, and furniture made of precious woods with Japanese silver, sandal wood, amber, aromatic woods, and incense from Indochina and spices from the islands of South Asia. It was a very vibrant little place. The porcelain, the silk, the precious woods furniture and the incense found its way into the simple décor of this magic place, inspiring visitors' lush dreams of Heaven's and Nature's beauty.

Ole opens in the early morning and it is then as well as in the evening that it is mostly frequented. The evenings were reserved for story-telling, music, and candle light poetry reading. Some were open for public and some had a special audience invited just for the occasion.

Amazing as only a dream can be, within this coffee shop patrons were more or less freed from the rigid protocols of our times. People varied, conversations varied, often uncovering deeper levels of philosophical truths, or Universal secrets. Since customers are free to choose their-own seating on the elevated platforms around the walls or on the floor that was in the winter covered in silky carpets, and colourful cushions, the exchange of thoughts, and the life-changing discussions often happened amongst strangers. The places were taken on the first come first served basis, not according to rank or wealth, creating a very exciting sense of freedom from any social constraint.

The art of making tea is called 'Cha Dao', said Ottavio standing amidst the ancient vases and jars, at a small carved wooden table performing the tea ceremony.

A good tea has the flavour of nature. It smells of the spring mountain waters, earth and air filled with cold breeze of winter that has just decided to leave us- added Ama, bringing some more porcelain tea caps. Get to know the tea plant to be able to bring out its most fragrant properties choosing the right pot, right amount of tea leaves, the right water temperature, the brewing time.

It was obvious from the enthusiasm that the father and daughter shared, and the shine in their eyes, that the ritual of preparing and serving tea had a special place in their lives.

The smell of tea, its taste, its texture, how smooth it is, how hot the mixture is, how refined the leaves are, and its right combination will bring out the perfection in it. Muttered Ottavio as thought he was talking about an alchemical process of changing metals into gold, not making tea.

He gently took the small porcelain cups from Ama cursing them in his large hand, placed them in a circle around a small, unglazed clay teapot made from red sand clay.

To seal the inside of the teapot, I boiled special old tea leaves mixture with water for many hours. Oils from the tea leaves sealed the pores of the fired clay and left a delicate scent that will stay with all our teas. An alchemist and a magician spoke to us about the sealing of the teapot.

"This is green tea", Ama continued, "the leaves of this tea are not broken, but dried into little buds, bringing the buds closer so I can smell them." The tender plants collected on the mountain hills looked alive in her beautiful gentle hands.

"What is the difference between black tea and green tea?" I asked, looking at the young, tender leaves in front of me.

"The difference is the length of the fermentation used to process the leaves."

"While fermenting, the green tea changes its colour into reddish-brown." She smiled. "The longer the fermentation, the darker is its colour."

"So green teas are just lightly fermented, I repeated while she nodded, "yes, the red and black teas could sometimes be fermented for years."

Ama left the tea leaves in my hands so I can touch them. Each step of this magical creation was for me a sensory exploration of a spiritual experience. The smell took me in to a journey to the high mountain ranges covered in mist untouched by a human foot.

After boiling water, Ottavio rinsed the teapot and cups with the steaming water. Each one of his movements was precise and meditative carrying within the respect for all the elements: fire, water, earth, air, respect for the tea and us, his guests at Ole. Using a bamboo tea scoop, he filled the teapot with tea leaves and then poured the boiling water into the pot to very quickly drain the water out.

"This dispels any bitterness", he says while rinsing and setting the tea leaves.

He poured the boiling water into the tea pot again and around 30 seconds later he poured the magic liquid into the cups moving the teapot around in a continual motion over the cups so that they are all filled together.

"The tea has to be poured low to minimize escaping of aroma and it is important not to have bubbles in the pot." He looked at me, as though he is telling me a secret of eternal life. "Bubbles, when mixed with the tea, form a foam that spoil its purity."

"Each cup should taste exactly the same and have the exact same colour," he noted.

Handing one of the cups to me I gracefully sipped the magic of this liquid. The tiny chalice is just large enough to hold about two small sips of the tea. The tea tasted much different than it smelled. It had a bitter, earthy, green-twig taste. Looking at the colour I observed a few leaves gently unfolding within my cup. Each time, I have entered the silence of meditation observing this little ritual.

The ceremony continued.

"Each pot of tea serves three to four rounds and the same tea leaves are used over again until the fragrance is gone." My host explained.

"China is the homeland of tea." I noted as they both nodded.

"We, for certain know that the Chinese had tea-shrubs five to six thousand years ago", Ottavio said.

"During the mid-Tang Dynasty (around 700 A.D) a Buddhist monk, Lu Yu, wrote the first Tea Classic. It was called Cha Ching, a script explaining and exploring the art of making tea. Ama loves this ancient script, maybe one of these evenings she could share it with you."

"Tea is very popular in China. In summer we cool ourselves drinking it, and in winter it warms us. We have a saying," Ama said smiling: "Rather go without salt for three days than without tea for a single day."

"Yes, I see constantly lots of old men gathering around teapots, talking," I said.

"This we call: Lao Jen Cha, Old Men's Tea ceremony, and probably we inherited it from our ancestors from 2,000 years ago," Ama added thoughtfully.

After the tea ceremony, Ama took me around their little coffee and tea house. She wanted to show me the gardens that were behind the gate, reserved for friends and blooming wonders in this spring day.

Walking through the gardens I could see that all the structures, bridges, fences and trails were designed in a most imaginative and refined manner. Weathering just gave a meaning to some of the areas crossing our paths.

The plants and the paths, all, take in the element of time with grace, old age and death is not frowned upon, here in China, it is respected. Ama was reading my thoughts.

The garden was built around a large pond.

"Water is an important element in Chinese life and it is almost always present in Chinese gardens," my beautiful host explored the elements with me. "Even in the dry gardens, you find water symbolized by grey gravel or sand with sand patterns on it."

In the centre of the pond was an island, "an island of immortals," Ama explained, "a large stone resembling a miniature mountain."

"Because of its sacred character, the island is no longer accessible to people, as you can see no bridges lead to it." Laughing is praying, so we laughed often.

The island was the shape of a tortoise, an animal that according to Chinese mythology lives ten thousand years and symbolises longevity, and there were no bridges leading to it, just a few small rocks placed around it, inviting visitors to hop from one to the other, giving them a hope that even though the sacred place is unapproachable.

"With an effort, one still can reach it and live everlasting happiness." I said.

Trees and plants planted all around the paths were also narrating stories. "Both the bamboo and pine as an evergreen," Ama pointed out, "express longevity and happiness."

"The black or male pine and red or female pine symbolize yang and yin forces of the universe. That is why they are planted next to each other, they could not exist without the other. The plum brings forth the qualities of vigour and patience since it blooms first after the cold winter months."

Further down the path, I noticed some large rocks with their main bodies set deep into the ground as though the gardener wanted to offer a symbol, a thought, a shape intriguing our minds, expanding beyond just the physical manifestation. I asked Ama about it.

"This garden is a shrine," she said. "We surround ourselves with shrines." Every stone, every tree, every pathway is a shrine." Looking around I saw a symbolism behind each pattern, each plant planted, and each colour chosen. "We build shrines everywhere, within the walls of our houses, at the entrance of our shops, at the corners of our streets and in the fields." Symbols, rituals and magic, were all in the core of our Being.

We entered their outdoor pavilion with a floor carved in the shape of a Chinese character. Through one of the carvings on the floor, surged a stream running from the pavilion to their rocky garden.

"Giving full respect tp all the elements," Ama said, "within an Egyptian Initiation, next to the great Sphinx of Thebes that has a head of a man, body of a lion, wings of an eagle, our ancestors worshiped the Water, Air, Earth, or Fire, stolen from Gods. The pre-structured resistance within all that is Form, a dragon-like creature that represents the Life Force itself. Throughout our mythology, the man swims through consciousness and subconscious layers of behaviour and within various artistic expressions, as a knight, he fights the Life Force, taming the Dragon with Knowledge and Light."

This thought brings my heart back to Pythagoras. "Bless us, divine number, thou who generated gods and men! O holy, holy Tetractys, thou that containest the root and source of the eternally flowing creation! For the divine number begins with the profound, pure unity until it comes to the holy four; then it begets the mother of all, the all-comprising, all-bounding, the first-born, the never-swerving, the never-tiring holy ten, the key holder of all." This is a Pythagorean prayer about Tetractys, smiled Ama reciting it by heart.

Yes, I also know of an ancient Pythagorean oath that mentions the Tetractys, I added:

"By that pure, holy, four lettered name on high,
nature's eternal fountain and supply,
the parent of all souls that living be,
by him, with faith find oath, I swear to thee."

The ancient Greek work always fascinated me the most. Hellenistic mathematicians in the 500 BC, preferred using a system of numbers based on the alphabet. To indicate that a letter is a number, they would place a horizontal line above the symbol. The Tetractys or Decad (for it has 10 numbers and letters included) is both a mathematical idea and a metaphysical concept.

1 or 10 or 10 of each number, or 1,0000 (one of 10,000) a number and sound frequency of supreme God.

If the Ancient Greek numerical system, had an alphabetic letters assigned to a number, researchers would get some most inspiring combinations, 241 as 200 + 40 + 1 would have been ΣMA or 666 is written as χξς (600 + 60 + 6) X-Đ-C, and philosophers would have explored the Saturn shift of frequency or energy from 6 "C" to 60 *Đ to 600 *X

"The symbol for "dragon" in Chinese is long 龍," she added showing me the symbol carved on a stone we passed, "associated with good fortune, traditionally having power over rain. Many East Asian deities have dragons as their companions. Do you know that the Emperor of China is the only one permitted to have dragons carved on his house, clothing, or personal articles?"
"Really? So how come you got these?" He pointed to a sculpture shaping the pond.

Not on the clothing though,
"The muš-uššu is a Mesopotamian dragon from Babylon with the body and neck of a snake, the front legs of a lion and the back legs of a bird." I recalled.

"Interesting," Ama smiled, "Chinese shamans are educated for decades, researching many different fields: weather forecasts, magical healing, dream interpretation, and fortune-telling, using astrology, sound healing or feng-shui, to communicate with Gods and spirits. The relationship between Chinese and their Gods is very personal."

I had to admit that for most of Europeans, Chinese culture was completely alien, yet I had a privilege to study Ancient Greeks, so I could contribute to this little discussion. Knowing Ama's deep fascination with Pythagoras, I told her: "Pythagoras gave the name of Monad (1) to God, and Dyad (2) to matter. The first and highest aspect of God is described by Plato as the One. The Monad (indescribable) emanated the Demiurge

(Tao, Consciousness, and Transcendent Source) or the creator. Plato, in the Socratic dialogue Timaeus, refers the Demiurge as a benevolent force that has created the world out of Chaos. Plotinus metaphorically identified the Demiurge as the Greek God Zeus (spelled as θεὸς or Δἰὸς) becoming "Dios" of the Catholic Roman Church.

Do you know how the Ancient Greeks spell the word "Goddess", I shared this spelling with Ottavio. θεα

Aristotle equated matter with the formation of the elements moved to action by force or motion. These two are known as Aristotle's Energeia and Plato's Demiurge.

The Demiurge of Neoplatonism is the Nous (mind of God), and it is:

1. Arche – "beginning" or the source of all things,
2. Logos – "reason" or the cause behind all,
3. Harmonia – "harmony" reflected with the Numbers in mathematics.

It would seem then that the Orphic view of the Demiurge was integrated into Jewish and Christian Gnosticism. Later within the Judeo-Christian tradition, the Demiurge or creator, became Lucifer or Satan with the firmly attributed evil to the concept of Creation, whereby God wishes to limit man's knowledge by forbidding him the fruit of knowledge in paradise, while within the teachings of Pythagoras and Plato there is no "lesser", or "worse" God creating Universe and Humankind, even though the Universe is in Chaos."

We returned to Ole to share a cup of 'coffee'.

"This is not my first time in a coffee shop." I took Ama's hand, "I came across these fascinating gathering places travelling across villages in Yemen, and Mokeya was the name of the places. There, they stand in an open country, before the other village huts, at the edge of the settlements, offering Kischer, a hot infusion of coffee-beans, to travellers. This hot and bitter drink was strange to taste at first but with the most amazing smell, a bit like black tea but with an earthy overtone to its taste. Back there, in Yemen, it was served in simple and beautiful earthenware cups with water that was given out gratis." At the very beginning of my encounter with this magic liquid, it took some time to adjust to the bitterness of the coffee taste, but later I got hooked to the smells of spices added to it, to the ceremony around its making, and to the sweet expectation while waiting for coffee beans to be roast and ground, and the warm feeling of expansion that followed the experience of drinking. Here, at Ole, in China, the drink is served in beautiful Chinese porcelain cups.

Ole is near water, has many windows, and two small private almost invisible galleries, with an amazing view into the endless blue, where I many times got lost contemplating the secrets of existence. Its front garden was accessible to all and it changed with the seasons, shaded by a huge tree, full of roses and flowers, offered us, who came there regularly, a performance of shades, with interlude of sounds.

"Our, Western world is a rational, intellectual world that exists within linear thoughts, formulas, and clear logic." My friend, Ottavio, started one of his usual discussions when he was surrounded with his friends. "It is what Chinese call the Solar, Male, Yang of the creation."

"Chinese however is intuitive and imaginative. It is the heart, filled with symbols, signs, sounds, and meditations. It is the Yin of the creation, the Moon, the Female child of the Universe."

"If it just could be achieved," my dear friend, he turned around to face me, as though he is telling me the secret of our great, great grandparents, "the merge of Yin and Yang, would lead us to perfection, uniting Solar and Lunar ways of thinking would lead us, humanity, to a new state of Consciousness."

"Has already been attempted some thousands of years ago. In our wish to relate to omnipotent, omniscience, and omnipresence God, we used art, music or poetry to express since Ratio has no unobstructed pathways towards Divine.

The mysticism as a life-long research and devotion to God through beauty, is within each one of Ancient Europe Neolithic structure. But it is not just beauty that surrounds them but their deep mystical connection to the sound, symbols and mini universes represented in each sound or word.

When meditating about our Neolithic ancestors, attempting to connect to the stones as portals, to higher knowledge, our ancestors have mastered symbols and have created the first portable ways to communicate with Gods of Death: writing signs and chanting."

"My research is within alchemy that wishes to see the carbon of the human soul that is now visible as graphite, transform into the one of a diamond. If it just could be achieved we could see an inner transformation of any metal to gold. The Alchemy of Humanity! So, tell me more about yours?

"The real mix and historical factual mess-up has started once the minds of Europe have equated Roman Empire with the area of Macedonia, or Greece or the Byzantine Empire. The Greek civilization was far more advanced than any we have known within this area, dates back to 1,000 BC, yet Babylon goes back to 2,000 BC, with ancient Danube Vincha going back to 5,000 BC. All in the same region, all carrying "pagan" devotion to Mother Earth, expressed within Slav languages with the sound Dj, Ch, Sh.

The Egyptian civilization, ruling the area pre 1 BC, was absolutely stunning, so fascinating that each Eauropean King had a team of scientists researching ancient Egyptian wisdom. The Babylonian empire, Ancient Greece, or the Danube civilization, all have existed and managed the region of the wider Mediterranean for thousands of years before Rome."

"Continue, continue," Ottavio said, pouring some more tea.

"My home town is SiRMiuM, and the so called sacred topography of the Balkans, the northern frontier of the Roman Empire, from the banks of the Danube to the Adriatic Sea, hides the most interesting Ancient European Civilizations.

You must remember the story of the three Roman co-rulers Galerius, Diocletian and Constantine the Great. Galerius worshiped Dionysus and has deified his mother Romula and himself. Dionysus is the ancient god of wine, fertility, theatre, and religious ecstasy. His Roman name was Bacchus. We find him as a God as early as 1500 BC, worshiped by Mycenean Greeks.

The idea of death and resurrection, the god's permanent aspiration to bring humans into the world of gods after making them immortal, is from there. Dionysus is the savior of souls and the one who bestows eternal life. Like Dionysus and his mother Semele who joined the gods at the Mount Olympus, the striving for liberation of the Dionysian cult is at the core of Ancient Greek spirituality. It is from the Dionysian rites that the idea of the soul related to the divine and the soul immortality was passed to Humankind."

"In Sirmium, while growing up, I used to play digging for gold in the archaeological sites of the area. Believe it or not, kids would collect all sort of ancient jars. The city got its nick-name as the city of martyrs."

"JeSu, the Son of God has been translated in many ways, in an attempt to keep the original authenticity of the name and sound. The real sound of the name was Y-SH (Ja=Š or I=SH) as in YaSha and it has meant exactly that: "I am SH", the sound, at the time, worshiped as the name of the Supreme Female / Sun God by all the monotheistic nations of Europe – JeWs were the Ya-Sch followers."

"Yet it is through the mystical Sh or X, that we seek enlightenment, it is the element that through love induces the higher states of consciousness, for the lady love tolerates not a FoRCeFuLL effort. In our not so distant and in our very distant past we have followed Ra (Sun / GoD / BoG / Dio) or Ma (Moon / H / Sha / S).

When times were good, they loved each other, when times were rough they resorted to violence against each other. One would even hide the script from the ignorant so to stop them from killing each other.
The followers of the one God believed in trinity, the power above the Ra and Ma story that has been called by many names, by different monotheistic religions.

In the name of Democracy, Justice, Equality, the researchers of all the branches from all the countries, call them to stop and announced the end of the Religion Violence, and end of the Chosen Ones. This was the main cause of all the European wars, which have been one long continues never ending story."

"The major philosophical question we face even today, is: can you kill for God?" Said Ama.

"Mo-She came back from Sacred Mount Sinai, the name suggests the followers of the Moon Sacred Temple, with a straight forward NO, that has since been changed into many different forms."

"Any substance, as an alchemist would tell you, whatever it is," continued Ottavio, "is what it appears to be, set just for a moment lost in eternity, by parameters of a given place, time, and given circumstances. Carbon could be graphite and diamond at the same time. When a human being is subject to hardship, and mistreatment, he could become a murderer, a thief or an abuser. How quickly before he becomes an animal? When one is treated with love, respect and care, how far can he develop?" Contemplated Ottavio.

"A human being could be studied by investigating a section of his liver or the brain, or observing the amazing matrix of soul's behaviour patterns," said Ama, moving swiftly through the space of the hall.

"What is better: to build our knowledge from individual broken segments forming a thousand pieced mosaic puzzle-that clearly obstructs our vision, ...or to follow the spiritual intuitive way that uncovers the secrets of the cosmos interwoven with a magic game of our own imagination?" Asked Ama.

"Is there a man on Earth who could manage to bridge the gap between the two, who will not get discouraged by the barriers of different languages or by the dogmas of their religions?" They both for a moment, so I thought, looked at me...

Like a fog, silence crept into my world, entered my mind through the breathing and became a part of my being.

Silence narrated a story of a deep profound longing planted within my soul at the gate of creation.

I became Ama's and Ottavio's friend soon after I arrived to Macao. Both their lives were veiled with mystery and encircled with many common folk's legends, I loved and deeply respected their freedom of speech and thought, unknown to many in this day and age.

As a wild wind that crosses the planes on a still summer day surprising everybody around, or a water whirlpool playing in the midst of a calm sea, immensely freed from pre-conditioning, and predjudices, and almost dogmatically against dogmas, they lived their lives in Macao where different religions co-existed.

Ottavio was versed in both Western and Eastern philosophies. It was his love for religious studies that inspired him to support the intellectual and artistic elite of Macao, gathering them at his coffee and tea house, at 'Ole', having endless discussions about God, Purpose of Life, Philosophy or Art.

The group that gathered around Ottavio and his daughter Ama, was a group full of weird scientists and artists, wonderful trouble makers, who loved their tea and coffee.

Ole is by no means a noisy, cluttered space. With its serene, simple, white washed walls, paved with soft stone, and furnishing that is kept to a minimum, scented with incense, and large windows facing the big blue ocean, lit by candles at night, its design talks magic about its owners Ottavio and Ama.

To the eyes of non-believers in this astonishing shift of ages, life still appeared the same, and yet, underneath this calm surface of the sea of the existence, a great transformation was taking place.

This evening we have just finished listening to Ama playing 'bianzhong', a heavenly instrument made of 65 bronze bells. Ama's hands played the bells as though each of her fingers possessed a brain on its-own with a magical, instinctive, intuitive feel that directs the music without any interference with the cold, intellectual and rational brain that exists up there, in the head. She took me on to a journey of phoenix sounds, rituals and tales of harmony only found in the sound.

After the performance, I examined this marvellous instrument that took me to such an inspiring spiritual journey.

An amazing three-tier frame carries the bells that are each different in size giving different sounds. The frame and the bells had Chinese characters engraved on them.

Ama told me that she is at the moment studying the 3,000 characters found on the instrument and that they are a treatise on ancient Chinese musical theory. The instrument was a gift from the Chinese Emperor and was made purposely for Ottavio as an exact replica of a 2,000 years old organ that is used by the court's musicians in creation of ritual and court music. The one that I was listening to was just 10 times smaller.

"This exquisite work of art largest bell is as high as myself," explained Ottavio, "and it weighs over 200 kg. Inscriptions are engraved with gold on each bell and its music capabilities are amazing... I watched five performers play the Royal set."

"This replica sounds just as amazing..." I remarked.

Ottavio is not a man much given to flattery but he couldn't hide a smile of pride for possessing such an art work.

"It is fascinating that virtually all major texts, whether philosophical, or poetic from old China are discussing music, music as an integral part of ritual activity, or music as a key to understanding Nature." Meditated Ama.
"A Soul or DuŠa in Slavic," I told them, "is on its mystical journey through sounds and their ffrequencies, and is influenced by them. A fairly early monotheistic notion, of one and supreme God to worship, was evident within the development of the Balkan Slavic languages, and it in its puzzling complexity ends with the supreme mystical story of the Holy Trinity."

"The Orthodox Christians have kept the secret of sacred sound and music within their own ritual practices. The most ancient description of Divine Liturgy is written in 138 AC by Justin the Martyr, a Christian saint, a well-studied man who in his Dialogue tells us of his early education, his theological and metaphysical inspiration coming from the philosophers of Stoic, Pythagorean and Plato schools. He refers to Sun-Day, as the Lord's Day, the day of Kyrios. The lingua franca used during the Late Bronze Age in the area was Akkadian." I offered my bit of exchange into this conversation.

"How interesting, music must have been used by all the ancient civilizations as the major tool to shift states of consciousness. Confucius, we are talking 500 BC, was convinced that music has a role in maintaining social order. His idea was that a musical system reflects the proper code of moral behaviour. In his view, Life is about 'wholeness' and music is able to demonstrate the importance of regularities and wholeness." Said Ama.

"Chinese have a great interest in studying the vibration of any instrument. They compare pitches to the configuration of cosmic Qi energy." Added Ottavio.

Ama's beauty engulfed me. Her fascination with the Chinese system of knowledge was infectious, leaving me in awe at the vastness and depth of knowledge opening accumulated by Humankind.

"The Chinese interest in music is an interest in numbers and symbols, not in quantification and absolute numerical value. Numbers are manipulated as symbols. The Chinese have an elaborate scheme of correlations, the 12 pitch scale is related to the 12 lunar cycles, and they created an elaborate edifice of relationships to interpret Nature, Humans and History." said Ottavio.

Early Chinese mystics tell us that 12 pitches are discovered by their sage Ling Lun with a name that means 'structure and order', he was a minister of the Yellow Emperor. Ling Lun observed the songs of the male and female phoenix, the male (yang) calls were six and the female (yin) were six. The legend says that these became pitches of the early music structure. The Yellow Emperor ordered Ling Lun to cast twelve bronze bells that sound the exact pitch. In the Chinese mind, this ordered symbolic set derived directly from observing Nature. Its pitch is an attribute of a lunar cycle. Under each moon, you will find zodiac recommendations and suggestions for human behaviour, and each pitch belongs to a particular lunar cycle.

Confucius believed that if you disturb the rightful order and structure, your mind is going to be disturbed. For example, he spoke of the music of Zheng comparing it to the colour - purple. Purple, is a combination of colours, a combination of red and blue. It detracts from the purity of red, and it does not have the depth of blue. He claimed that the music of Zheng was not in harmony with the elegant ritual music of ancient China, and that this only reflected the state's government that was deviant and wicked.

"It is an astonishing shift of ages that we live in, isn't it?" Ama said.

The astrological and prophet texts published all throughout the 16th century led to the same conclusion: that the end of our World would be with us, if not the next morning, then surely in the couple of years. The astrological tables have predicted an unusual succession of eclipses at the very start of the 17th century and numerologically the year 1600 was the chosen year: 16 being the number that was composed of seven and nine, the divine numbers by hundred times, multiplying its magical fatal value.

Ottavio laughed at this belief.

Soon after he arrived to Macao, Ottavio publically exhibited his good will towards the Church and City Council supporting the foundation of St. Paul's College, which was the first European University in China. The College offered courses in European Arts and Theology and simultaneously concentrated on the studies of the Chinese and Japanese language and civilisation.

With his never-ending fortune he heavily financed this project. Just after he had given me a substantial amount of money for building one of University Halls, pouring Chinese tea into my cup, he said:

"It is quite amazing how a culturally and scientifically inferior nation took upon itself a mission to convert a superior one. Missionaries would love to convince the Chinese to worship the *Right God*, his voice slightly changed emphasising the absurdity of this term, even though this IS a supreme dogma that puts God into a box that does not allow expressions of spiritual diversity amongst different nations. If there is anything that will destroy the Church, and Religions, it will be this selfish attitude of every one of them that keeps the right to God only to its followers!"

It was very difficult to win an argument with Ottavio, he was more or less always right, quick with words, hard with fakes and hypocrites. Honest and truthful to the core creating many rivals.

His enemies within the Church have often questioned my relationship with him, but with my easy access to his wealth, their greediness superseded their worry and his heretical behaviour dispersed amongst the golden shine of his coins.

Speculations about Ottavio's fortune were many, speculations about murders, devils, inheritance, and wicked businesses, but no one could really tell anything specific about Ottavio's past and his wealth: he only joked about it. Trying my luck this time, asking him about alchemy and his fortune, his answer was as mysterious as he:

"With alchemy, my dear friend, I DID learn how to make gold," he said. Using alchemy, any metal can become gold, and any human can reach his highest potential. "The coffee beans become gold," he looked at me with a devilish smile, "I work with both, metal and people, and people my dear friend, are much more challenging!"

Alchemy is a science that fascinated many for centuries. Scientists would spend hours and hours of sleepless nights examining and experimenting with the nature of chemicals in hope to find the sacred stone that transforms metals to gold.

Ottavio tried a few times to pass some of his enthusiasm towards Alchemy.

"Alchemy and Astrology, it is said in the old scriptures, are two of the eldest sciences known to mankind passed to us from the prehistoric times. According to old Rabbins legends, the two arts were divinely revealed to Adam, promising that when the human race masters the wisdom concealed within them, the curse of the forbidden fruit will be removed."

Astronomy and alchemy were the most sacred secret of the Atlantis priests. Apparently, when Atlantis was destroyed, the art was passed to Egypt and then to Europe. The sages and philosophers created an intricate allegory of symbols to conceal their wisdom.

"Personally, I believe that all the ancient secrets were passed through the sounds." I explained, "The Lord's Prayer in Greek is: "ΠΑΤΕΡ ΗΜΩΝ Ο ΕΝ ΤΟΙΣ ΟΥΡΑΝΟΙΣ ΑΓΙΑΣΘΗΤΩ ΤΟ ΟΝΟΜΑ ΣΟΥ ΕΛΘΕΤΩ Η ΒΑΣΙΛΕΙΑ ΣΟΥ ΓΕΝΗΘΗΤΩ ΤΟ ΘΕΛΗΜΑ ΣΟΥ, ΩΣ ΕΝ ΟΥΡΑΝΩ ΚΑΙ ΕΠΙ ΤΗΣ ΓΗΣ ΤΟΝ ΑΡΤΟΝ ΗΜΩΝ ΤΟΝ ΕΠΙΟΥΣΙΟΝ ΔΟΣ ΗΜΙΝ ΣΗΜΕΡΟΝ ΚΑΙ ΑΦΕΣ ΗΜΙΝ ΤΑ ΟΦΕΙΛΗΜΑΤΑ ΗΜΩΝ, ΩΣ ΚΑΙ ΗΜΕΙΣ ΑΦΙΕΜΕΝ ΤΟΙΣ ΟΦΕΙΛΕΤΑΙΣ ΗΜΩΝ ΚΑΙ ΜΗ ΕΙΣΕΝΕΓΚΗΣ ΗΜΑΣ ΕΙΣ ΠΕΙΡΑΣΜΟΝ, ΑΛΛΑ ΡΥΣΑΙ ΗΜΑΣ ΑΠΟ ΤΟΥ ΠΟΝΗΡΟΥ. ΑΜΗΝ." I sung
"The sacred Egyptian SH, later became W, in English, has changed its form into the Greek Σ, S of the Latin Spirito Santos, as early as within the translations of the script of the Ancient Greeks, hiding the SH vibration of Isis, the Death, the Underworld, Night, Meditation, MiNoS, Mum, Nirvana, Death, Sub consciousness, or the YiN of Consciousness that has in the Ancient Europe lost its potency with the loss of sounds such as Ž or Đ or Š or DŽ or Č."

"There is no CH as in Cheese or as in ČoNo in Slavic languages, or Church in English, in the Greek language, so the first translation of any ancient text into the Ancient Greek Θ or ῶ. or Σ or Μ, got a different sound. CH always sounds like K. At one point of our history, within the Ancient Egyptian, Ancient Hebrew, Ancient Geez, all the names of Gods, influential people, Kings or Phaereos carried the sounds of Ž Đ Č, DŽ or SH, and all the sound rituals were conducted with this magic Tibetan Budhist deep male musical scale and was contrasted with the female angelic sounds of N and M sung with vowels through the Greek Ἀ μὴν ΑΜΕΝ or ΑΜΟΝ or ΑΜΙΝ." ψάλλει τὸ Κύριε, is - In peace, let us pray to the Lord or = ShaLoM with Siii, KiRiJe (bless-me with S or Š)

"It is like speaking a Universal language, the language of Gods, the first language, understandable to all!"

As a philosopher, I knew that passed through pictures, like the ancient Egyptian spirituality, whether Christians, Muslims or Hindus, Taoist, Jews, Atheists or Buddhists, our scientists, applied psychologists and consciousness researchers, always followed their inner-most drive for goodness as their souls' quest, no matter what their have chosen as their personal growth system. This was my description of Alchemy.

So, the whole world of mythological creatures was a gift of conscious and unconscious learnings and some exceptionally talented scientists of the last 200 years devoted their lives to translate these works.
I've seen him transform many times.

Ottavio and me shared the same fascination with the glorious lady Knowledge, people's little peculiarities and weaknesses did not quite amuze him.

"I am a heretic, my dear friend Benedict, all these books make you one." Ottavio looked into my eyes, nodding "but all the knowledge in the world is useless if we do not act consciously, understanding the consequences of our actions and thoughts."

"Can we ever hope to understand the consequences of our actions to the lives of the people that will live many, many centuries later?" I asked, not hoping for an answer.

Did Christ know that his teaching will be used and abused during the centuries of religious wars? Did Moses know that 1,000 of years later we will still struggle to understand his main command: do not kill! Does everything happen for a reason?

That evening we were invited to a dinner and treated to a variety of delicious vegetarian dishes.

Each dinner at Ole was a carefully prepared master piece. An amazing variety of wholesome Chinese treats teased our taste buds.

Each dish was presented in exquisite porcelain wares, Ottavio's gifts from various courts. The fineness of the porcelain with delicacy of the paintings were impressive.

The elegant deep blue flying-fish dragons writhing against storming waves stared at us passing their wishes for good fortune, long life, immortality, and plenty. Peaches represent immortality, pomegranates symbolize fertility, and apples are a homonym for peace, were all greeting us symbolically, this time when we sat around for the dinner.

Drinks were in porcelain jugs in a form of women playing instruments with the divine fruit nectars pouring out through their hands, reminding us of the importance of music.

Veggie fried rice, bright, crisp and spicy Chinese beans, tasty steamed buns, fragrant ginger and lemongrass flavour vegetable salads, young, thin beans that are tossed in soy sauce with fresh ginger in a stylish side dish, roasted tofu deliciously browned and flavoursome, little rice and sesame pancakes with a topping of a crunchy salad of nuts, marinated red cabbage and Chinese salad leaves. All of these magical dishes were performing a séance in its own right.

At first we indulge in the tastes, smells, and textures, to be soon released into the waters of mental endeavour.

After the meal, finding myself in front of Ottavio's amazing library, I picked a book randomly, caressing its leather covers. The printing press brought a complete revolution into our worlds: I was witnessing the huge expansion of knowledge amongst the educated classes all across different cultures.

The book in my hands was *Malleus Maleficarum* otherwise known as Witches' Hummer, the book that became fundamental for superstitious gibberish of millions of people who believed in witches.

"Did Pope Innocent know what kind of effect he would have on masses before he drafted his decree talking about witches?" I asked showing the book to Ottavio.

"Did the Dominican monks that wrote Witches' Hummer knew that the book will become the largest executing manual of any times?" "Do the first two superstitious witnesses, accusing their neighbours of witch-craft, know that their accusation will spread like fire and eventually cause the death of their own daughters and their own mothers?" Asked back Ottavio holding the book.

I wasn't the only priest that disagreed with this book and the methods used by the Inquisition to torture innocent women. It was a matter of a constant debate amongst us within the Monastic Order and I became very angry every time somebody supported it. The fact that we were so far away from the main-land Europe made my resistance to these hateful, and despiteful acts possible.

"A Confucius' would say that it is a man that makes the Way great." Ottavio said in anger, talking about the manual, angered him.

"It is man that can change and shape the history. We are not peons, or some sort of victims, we are staging this little performance called life."

"What a horrible book, a burning manual!"

A typical craze would start with one or two suspects and through the forced confessions would spread indefinitely taking 100s and sometimes 1,000s of innocent, the longer the panic lasted, the larger the numbers and wealthier the victims.

Treading the path of the development of Human Thought, giving full respect to Mother Philosophy and acknowledging how difficult it is to implement any noble idea in the world where Peace as Humanity highest Potential is still a very far goal, I was in owe of leaders who were introducing democracy within their city states 100s of years before Christ.

In search of perfection, veneering many centuries of struggle for equality, researching consciousness, and the arena of alchemy of human society, some of the most amazing social experiments and their implementation by exceptional souls were born around the Mediterranean, more than 2,000 years ago.

"Look at all the discoveries of those young and excited minds that are galloping freed from their cages of centuries of Dark Age!" I could hear someone say.

"So many Souls have descended to guide us through this transition. So many books have been published that break our current beliefs, so the new ones will be born from their ashes."

Somebody picked up Campanella's book and started reading: *Truth can be hidden and persecuted, but it cannot be held prisoner by injustice; in the end it emerges from the darkness and is once again resplendent.*

As a priest, writer, and a professor, I had an access to works of Campanella, Copernicus, Giordano Bruno and I admired their fight with dogmatic systems within the Church.

Giordano was one of my teachers and his work inspired me greatly. A well-travelled, well-educated priest that lived in Switzerland, France, England and Germany, translating books, lecturing, and wherever he could, announcing the new view of the Universe.

Picking up 'De la Causa, Principio e Uno' I started reading Giordano Bruno's contemplations of God:

'The absolute potential is one, the act is one, the form or soul is one, the material or body is one, the thing is one, the being in one, one is the maximum and the best.. It is not generated, because there is no other being it could desire or hope for since it comprises all being. It does not grow corrupt because there is nothing else into which it could change, given that it is itself all things. It cannot diminish or grow, since it is infinite.'

"Our amazing culture gave birth to the likes of Giordano Bruno." I whispered thoughtfully.

"Giordano spoke of the infinity of the universe," whispered back Ottavio, turning his head towards the starry night.

"So, he says that we are not alone... An Italian, I've heard?" Smiled Ruben.

"He lived all over the world, in Switzerland, France, England, Germany, worked as a translator of many inspiring books, lecturing, and wherever he could, announcing the new view of the Universe. I was talking about a man who inspired me greatly, so I happily took a role of a narrator about his amazing work and his unfortunate destiny."

"A life of a travelling scholar and a lecturer, I wouldn't mind that type of life." Ruben added.

"Giordano was a Christian?" Somebody asked.

"Yes, a Dominican friar, but he saw the Church teachings as entirely irrational, based on no scientific basis. He believed in an infinite universe which had left no room for Christian God that was solely occupied with Earth and humans. His philosophy made the mystery of the virgin birth meaningless, and he thought that only the ignorant could take the Bible literally." Ottavio joined our discussion with a zest of a true heretic.

"His integrity and the lack of compromise towards his ideas got him imprisoned and he spent six long years in the dark dungeons of a Papal prison." I continued the story. "And yet, when threatened by the death sentence Giordano answered: "Perhaps you, my judges, pronounce this sentence against me with greater fear than I receive it.".

"Perhaps you, my judges, pronounce this sentence against me with greater fear than I receive it." Repeated Ruben thoughtfully.

"Is it true that he was the leader of an underground movement?" Asked Ottavio.

"That I don't know, but what I know is that he was a prophet whose thoughts changed the world bringing about a cosmological and moral revolution." Said Ruben.

"Killed as a heretic, burnt by the Inquisition in Campo di Fiori in Rome in 1600." Ottavio offered the un-happy ending.

A brief silence covered the room. The faces around the fire were contemplating the life and work of a man who was not alone, but had to die because he was the first one to publically challenge and disapprove the obvious.

"The ancient thought, that universal orbits must be circular, was not a new re-discovery for Europe," I said.

"Ancient Greece, between 800 BC and 100 BC saw most amazing advances in art, philosophy and science, and it was the age of city-states or polis that had own Local Governments, free of Global Taxes, protected by own Gods, for hundreds of years.

This was the time when science and religion were not separate and getting closer to the Truth (In Search of Truth) meant getting closer to the Gods. Classical Greece is considered to be the seminal culture or the cradle of Western civilization.

Just to give you an idea of how advanced this civilization was, Pythagoras and his students Plato, and Aristotle, both coming from Athens, understood the importance of symbols, numbers, or mathematics as instruments of Universal Truth that offer divine knowledge following the main Macro manifesting within Micro principle. Pheidon of Argos established a system of weights and measures, Theagenes of Megara brought running water to the city. Homer produced his Iliad and Odyssey, found later in the rich Egyptians Mummy burial cases, sculptors created statues as memorials to the dead, Anaximandros devised a theory of gravity; Xenophanes wrote about his discovery of fossils; and Pythagoras discovered his Pythagoras theorem.

As farming villages grew larger, they developed their own Governments and organized their inhabitants around set of laws. They all had economies that were based on agriculture. These city-states were known as poleis and were protected by own Gods or Goddess,

Athens and Sparta were both protected by Athena or perhaps I shall call her aXeN. Most had overthrown their hereditary kings, or priests, and each of these poleis was an independent city-state. The new poleis were self-governing and self-sufficient. The new emerging polies were not politically controlled by their founding cities.

Following the Classical period was what is known as the Hellenistic period during 300 to 100 BC, during which we find Alexander the Great within Babylon walls.

This classical period also brought with it a political reform known as "demokratia", or "rule by the people."

"By the 6th century BC Greece had influential Governments: Athens, Sparta, Corinth, Thebes and Argos. Athens and Corinth also became major maritime powers. In this period, the advent of the democracy of Athens led to a 'golden age' for the Athenians. They spread Greek art and initiated a creative revolution. and it spread around scientific circles very quickly, notwithstanding the dangers of the Church." This time it was Ama talking.

"Despite the threat of the Inquisition, Galileo Galilei, another great man and scientist, after his discovery of an astronomical telescope and his detailed researches, publishes revolutionary prints describing the motion of the Earth around the Sun." Ruben was back to the Age of Reason.

"You are talking about the *Dialogue Concerning the Two Chief World Systems,* isn't it?" Asked Ottavio. After he has published this work, the Inquisition quickly declared his views absurd and arrested him."

"You are fortunate to be living in China." I turned towards Ottavio. "Otherwise you would have had the same faith." I smiled at my dear friend.

"For sure," laughed Ottavio, "a witch, a wizard, a magician, an alchemist, or simply a man who is not afraid to question, and 'these' are the worst!" "Also, I would not wish to stay anywhere else, my dear friend, this is where everything IS happening!"

"We find the Ancient Egyptian name of God in Greek translations to be: NΘR sounding a bit like the Ancient Chinese Taoist Tao Te Ching story of Yi (as one) that has created aR (as two) and SaN (as three), while Babilonian speak of all talk about the same Theological concept of Trinity of sounds and frequencies that have carried the manifestation into Being, as female and male."

"A bit like Chinese…" Ama added.

"We find the Ancient Egyptian name of the Supreme God written as nHr or nTr or nDr (sounds of X for Xristos, Đ for Jay, and Č for chakra or čovek in Slavic) symbolically represented as a moving X, a spiral, a snake, a Kundalini moving wheel, the Supreme Goddess."

"Our ancestors were supreme masters in sound frequency, when they gave us symbols, or sounds, they did it for they had a complete science / theology within their mysticism and magic, in mind. Treat them as the most educated researchers of the Humanity History, perhaps 0.001% of humanity, who were trying to pass their knowledge to us. The Ancient Egyptians for example speak of the sounds that is used to change the energy from one to the other, so they call Gods; H or D or T pronouncing them as X, or Đ, or Č, allowing the soul to take the quality of the sound of Gods. For example the sounds R or B carry within its sound Ra, BoDy or BuDHa, Dio, the enlightened one. Bu in Chinese means towards the divine, Bu taking the sound of the name for the Soul in Ancient Egypt, or the number eight in China, infinity, meaning also a prophet, a God in making, symbolically represented as the cross + Yi (that is one) - + I (descending form heaven) to form a human soul that is blessed by the Divine Spirit."

"Fascinating!" Ama was the first one to break the silence.

"So that is why the Church increased the use of the censorship with its list of forbidden books, the *Index Librorum Prohibitorum*" asked Ottavio turning to Ruben.

"You are talking to the converted, I strongly disagree with the Church that is blessing slaughters in the name of God." Ruben agreed.

"Our task is for sure, to find where the balance between the two is, between the science and spirituality on Earth." Ottavio nodded. "Now this IS a difficult task."

"Science and spirituality are so intrinsically different that it is impossible to establish peace amongst them." Ruben kept contemplating.

"Male and female side of God's creation, Yang and Yin of Nature, mental and emotional side of human mind, the supremacy of any one causes the destruction of Balance and Harmony." Ama's hands danced a sort of tai-chi dance, her beautiful figure moved and hands circled their way into harmony to visually announce this eternal truth.

"Who could possible understand the Way?"

This is the time when I was re-discovering the writings of 'pagans': Greek, Roman and Egyptian philosophers, whose works were re-published, bound in silk, and revived after centuries of neglect.

The truth revealed in these texts went beyond the fashion of manuscript searches and hunts for undiscovered classics.

The Philosophy of our age is tightly connected to the Old and New Testament, but with the discovery of press and re-discovery of Greek and Latin texts, the scientific minds of our era got challenged, and opened to the new ideas.

At that moment I was reading Metamorphoses. Transformation. an epic poem in fifteen books written 2,000 years ago, by the Roman poet Ovid, completed in 8 AC. The poet's writings are based on already fully established Ancient Greek manuscript tradition, re-writing myths, the creation story, Ovid begins by describing how the elements emerge out of chaos, and how mankind degenerates from the Gold Age to the Silver Age to the Age of Iron. This is followed by an attempt by the giants (Titans) to seize the heavens, at which the God "Jove" sends a great flood which destroys all living things except one couple, Deucalion and Pyrrha.

The Metamorphoses, as a collection of myths is influenced by an earlier Greek work called the Theogony Θεογονια "Birth of the Gods" attributed to Hesiod 700 BC where Hesiod describes how the gods were created, their struggles with each other, and the nature of their divine rule. In the Theogony, the origin (arche / aRČe) is Chaos, a primordial condition, a gaping void (abyss), with the beginnings and the ends of the earth, sky, sea, gods, and mankind. Symbolically associated with water, it is the source, origin, or root of things that exist. Then came Gaia (Earth), Tartarus (the cave like space under the earth), and Eros, who becomes the creator of the world. The majority of the hymns celebrate the twelve Olympians gods and goddesses who dwell on Mount Olympus. In ancient Greek philosophy, arČe is the first principle of all things. Thales (700 – 600 BC), claimed that the first principle of all things is water.

In the Babylonian creation story Enûma Eli-Š (great Š), the universe was in a formless state and is described as a watery chaos. From it emerged two primary gods, a male and a female, and a third deity: the maker Mummu.

My meditations were interrupted by Ama's question: "Have you seen Leonardo's and Michelangelo's anatomical drawings that show their close study of human remains?"

"Yes, they are pretty amazing, some of the taboos of our era are constantly shaken." Ottavio's eyes were shining. "Human dissection, for scientific studies is now accepted and became a part of the scientific studies of different Universities enhancing our chemistry, medicine, and human anatomy."

"Standing at the entrance of the 16th century, Leonardo Da Vinci's life is another example of the life of an ideal 'Renaissance man', an all-round genius, a painter, a sculptor, a scientist, an architect, a philosopher and a spiritual teacher with ideas that were far ahead of his time." Ama narrated this story. Leonardo was a man she admired greatly.

"Leonardo is an inventor with the mind set deep in the future and the body living here, amongst us. His designs of flying machines, flour mills, and different engines, including a bicycle are not of this time." Said Ruben.

"A very inspiring soul, I heard he played the lyre..." Ottavio remarked.

"Not just that, he was an expert in botany, discussing war strategies with the soldiers and the nature of life with the truth seekers. His observations of the motions of the stars, the path of the moon, and the course of the sun are quite remarkable." Said Ama.

"A bit like you!" Laughed Ottavio...

Leaving Ottavio's place that day, walking through the streets of Macao, I contemplated the best ways to transfer these inspirational stories and thoughts into my day-to-day life.

Sunlight covered the Ocean and the twilight brought magic into my vision, I saw petals closing their home for the day, and ants hurrying back into their nests, saying good-night to each other, and wind whispering through the branches its lullaby to the birds and I strongly felt that we, humans, are just a fraction of this miracle called life. The night time crawled upon me and I dived into the vastness of the stars above me, sensing their infinity, and their eternity, reflecting our own unimportance.

Seeing myself as a mathematician, a scientist, and researcher, the dogmas presented to me by my Church have never really interested me. Reading manuscripts of some of the most amazing minds that argued that Earth is not the centre of the Universe and that we, human beings, are not the only sentient beings in this vast space, convinced me of how unimportant we actually are.

Long time ago, somewhere deep within my brain, God lost his long white beard, and his role of a parochial father that watches over his flock and counts their sins.

How small and insignificant we are. I talked to the flower.

The importance Christianity gave us was obviously exaggerated but un-importance that was opening in front of my eyes within this matrix of millions and millions of stars and billions of lives was dragging me into the oblivion of passivity, depression, and darkness.

To bring the life back into my bones, I needed a mission, I needed a purpose, a reason for living on this planet. I knew, both Ama and Ottavio had a mission and they both truly wanted me to become an essential part of it.

Love is life.
All, everything that I understand, I understand only because I love.
Everything is, everything exists, only because I love.
Everything is united by it alone.
Love is God, and to die means that I,
a particle of love,
shall return to the general and eternal source.
Leo Tolstoy

A Man Training To Love

Ama is an embodiment of every man's desires. She is our dreams of a perfect mother, a perfect lover and a perfect companion. A gentle pearl hidden in an oyster shell for such a long time that it became amazingly precious. Enchanted by her appearance, the sound of her voice, her scents, before I knew it, my soul biggest dream became to get lost in her arms, falling into the tender, loving light of her presence.

When I realised I am in love, it was way too late for any struggle my mind might have wished to put up. The love I felt for Ama was the deepest and closest feeling I have ever experienced to the feeling of complete devotion I felt for Christ and his teaching. Loving Ama was the closest I have ever been to God.

She entered into my worlds as a storm, and for months, perhaps even years, within me, there was no place for anything else while she was around.

I saw her during the day time, in the market, in front of the convent, in the midst of people, in the temples, in the sacred secret places, everywhere. I saw her when I was away, on my missions, within the shadows of unknown women cast on the walls of ruined houses, smiling at me from the statues of Chinese Goddesses, in the shape of lotus petals floating in the lake, within the silhouette of stones on my way to the Collage, in my dreams, and in my dreams...

If you were ever in love, you might understand the madness my mind was going through, the constant whisper that followed me through the sleepless nights, the hope to catch a glimpse of her fearing some might notice my fixation with her stories, habits, thoughts and dreams. Being a priest in love, just deepened my excitement and enchantment with this special soul, and prolonged my agony of consciously admitting that the butterflies in my stomach and my profound adoration to all she said or did, was my flesh's response to the Amor's arrow that found its way deep into my subconscious mind.

Convinced that I know my path, I walked steadily, not giving up, with the force only a man with completely set beliefs could have. A steady iron box was my life.

"The box that is around you during the last 20 years," Ama said jokingly, "is very hard to break".

The chemistry inside my brain wedged wars against my neurons and their well-established path-ways. My princess was wide awake and pain-strikingly conscious of her prince's darkness and fears. Still fully dressed in my warrior's armour ready to protect her from her sins, I got a bit confused by her lean, thin figure elegantly floating through the air, by her mind full of mental acrobatics that skilfully transformed my efforts to 'convert her' into little explosions of many dogmas within my heart. Afraid to touch her, in case my earthy touch breaks the spell and makes her vanish, disappearing into the realms of angels, I moved a step back.

"What about your emotions," she asked teasingly, "can they be, with an expert help, rounded or are they also square?"

A warrior without an armour, shy, clumsy and soft in her presence, "mould me", deeply longing to abandon the role of the spiritual teacher disappearing into her arms and her amazing Lightness of Being.

"The feelings I have for you," I told Ama, "are not sexual, I feel the purity of the spiritual connection between us."

The two of us became friends in a spontaneously loving moment of laughing, a laughter that hurt me because I did not know what to do with it.

"Ruben, how can you talk about sexuality, when you were celebrate all your life? The only thing that you know about sex is what is written within your manuals that condemn sex. The connection between our souls feels ever-lasting, spiritual and intense. The sexual energy is a gift from God and it is embedded within our human core for a reason, exploring it can be the most beautiful way to merge with Spirit. Taoist believe that joining the Essence is the most profound spiritual experience."

Ama took my hand and caressed it with utmost gentleness.

Some months later I told her: "I don't need the physical contact with you to feel complete," caressing curls of her hair. Just breathing the air you breathe is enough to open my heart.

If I lied at that moment it was purely because I did not know of other realities, because I truly believed that the sin of carnal lust and the subtle worlds of love are set apart by the widest and deepest gap imaginable.

The flow passing through me was precious, vibrant and its vitality re-discovered me. This delicate vibration could sustain me without any food or movement for hours and days.
I was in love.

During my mornings' walks I was able to see a conscious ant struggling to find its way through the maze determined to stop Earth from turning its seasons into a deadly winter that might kill his entire family.

Seeing a sparrow in love building the most amazing nest for his lover choosing a tree next to the Church, I felt the desire for Ama awakening within my soul descending from the dream's astral worlds to the terrestrial spheres. I respected the energy that was awakening within me over and over again, that brought to me a physical sensation of thousands of roaring lions, and at the same time, filled my heart with the soft and fluid touch of the lady Love.

Examining petals or my hands, sometimes for hours, admiring God's creations, slowing down, my soul wondered within the softness of the clouds of my imagination. Imagining her walking, talking, dancing, and disappearing into the Light. Pondering around her words like a bee around a flower, for days, keep returning to experience the essence of its nectar, I was powerfully self-absorbed, obsessed at times, not absent though, still able to meet people truly. The Lady Love actually opened me to God and His creation.

Her touch went deep through my skin, deep into the core of my being, in my bowels, in my stomach, in my spine.

She was taking me into the space of not breathing, not moving, into the space of the most amazing contact.

Dark Blue was the world around me, Dark Blue that took me to the end and the beginning of all known creation. Dark Blue were her feet, her eyes, her body and our merge that was reflected on the iron mirror opposite the bed that refused to know any boundaries, that jumped through the illusion of time taking the dimension of space-less-ness. Dark Blue was my first cum that shacked the Earth awaking my ancestors that were peacefully asleep for centuries. Dark Blue were my feelings of re-discovery of my-Self through the most amazing disappearing, burning every single cell of my body that wanted to keep re-collection of my personal history. Dark Blue was her stomach and the silk that covered it that I kept kissing lost within all possible realities of the form and being.

A man within me, the one with a strong personal history, strong habits and beliefs, a man in a box, felt the box rattling under a tremendous pressure keeping within a Soul that was yearning for freedom.

"I believe in what I preach," I told Ama, when our naked bodies have separated from the eternal embrace, and when I had enough time to forget the contact we just had, and enough strength to talk.

At that moment, when my mind kicked in again, I almost ought to feel guilty, I feel that everything that I 'am' needs to give itself another try, another push-through this weird and unknown territory.

I wanted to say, I murmured, "I do believe in what I preach."

She looked at me with no words, and her eyes gave me no choice but to disappear in them, again fully, for to love her, was to love the rest of humanity.

Vanishing, I have accepted that I am pure love, beautiful flowing Love. We merged again into a motion that became time-less, into an Essence that had no name or form other than Light. Our bodies swayed within the dance of creation known and unfortunately unknown to many, kept returning to its sacred secrets, kept exploring the prime-ordeal merge.

"Am I still a man I used to be?" I asked hours later. "Can I go back to the Monastery and live what I used to live?" I do love my God and Jesus, and just a moment ago, I had a Church that I called mine, and my Church said, very clearly,
that I ought to believe in mortal sins and
      the forgiveness of sins,
and my Church clearly defined me as a sinner and it said
      that I should ask for forgiveness and yet,
      now I know, the only thing I could feel at the moment of our Union, is the highest experience of Love.

Two Rubens now lived within me, one that finds thoughts and arguments a trivial pursuit of bored souls, happy within the Silence he explores the wonders of Life endlessly, and the other who is more argumentative, who is not sure what is the essence of his fight and why did God put him on Earth. This question became an irresolvable question that kept hunting the second Reuben: why did God give me this path?

Through experiencing Love, I lost Purpose, the purpose that led me to choosing the priesthood, the purpose that led me to China, and the purpose that guided my life since I was thirteen, the purpose of helping people understand Christianity and get closer to God. Finding

Ama, I could no longer say what my mission on Earth was.

Giving me Love, God has taken away from me all I knew, all I believed in, all I previously fought for.

One night, after an amazing merge with Ama that lasted for hours, I fell asleep in the Temple, and a woman appeared in my dreams standing above my head-rest. Her name was Purpose.

Remember, She said, touching my forehead, that Life is not just a string of days to be lived mechanically. They are our attempt to awaken and arouse the divinity in us. If you live with the full awareness, love could take you into this space.

To receive this most precious gift, you will have to let go of what is the most dear to you, to start a new, you will have to let go of the old, to fully Be, you will have to die and get re-born again.

A cupid appeared from nowhere whizzing his message.

She appears from nowhere, he said, and if you are not careful she will disappear as fast as she came into your life.

She takes your heart, your mind, your body, she juggles them, in an infinite play.

To test you, she brings her brothers jealousy, passion and desire into Her dance and if you are not careful she will leave you because of your attachment to her family.

If you take her into the mud of your existence, she will fool you and in front of your eyes disappear, wither and die. Carrying a veil of death in her hands she will either devour your-own earthly state, or the divine essence of Her own being. Giving you a gift of the Universal birth if only you could keep her alive for long enough, she will take you into the fullness of awareness. She will shake you into fully experiencing Life, into understanding God.

That night I woke up with a fever wishing to shake off the words that I've just heard, to push them into the subconscious darkness of my worst worries, to help them disappear into oblivion of someone else's consciousness, but they did not want to vanish.

It is not difficult to love, I thought, caressing the grass under my feet, Nature loves while it breaths. Love is all around.

My Being is filled with Love, how can it be that this profound feeling, this indestructible state of being, could ever disappear, could ever be forgotten or changed or misused, taken for granted, abused?

Afraid even to think that I could ever let go of this mesmerising beauty I looked into my future.

And something or somebody whispered into my ears:

afraid to lose her,
afraid to hurt her,
afraid to lose her, afraid to disappoint her,
afraid to lose her,
fear will kill your love, kill your love, kill your love...

A river materialised in front of me. A rain drop carried by a cloud circling above mountains, getting absorbed by a source, moving livelier and livelier, into a stream, uniting with other streams with the same goal, to reach the river, following the current, becoming a larger magnetic attraction aiming towards greater, finer, higher, stronger, vaster, so often dreamt of, and yet completely unknown, so well imagined and yet never experienced, reaching towards the sea. When my drop was certain that it cannot get bigger nor better any more, the sea merged with another forming an ocean. At one point all the oceans came together and became one big mass of water on Earth. What an amazing journey!

My drop carried within, all along, from its birth, a possibility to become a part of something greater. All along the way, there was a chance that it will disappear or evaporate going back to the cloud becoming a drop of rain again, starting the journey from the very beginning without reaching its ultimate end. All along the way, there was a possibility of a trap, a possibility of entering an endless circle of change and transformation, the drop that was never the same and yet always was – One.

One night we were sitting together looking each other deep into the eyes. Touching ever slightly, my palms were lost in hers. My breath followed hers disappearing within the flow of Her amazing Lightness of Being, and she took me into non-breathing, non-existence, into the core of Life.

Vibrating with every cell of my Being this sacred flow, my mind was lost in the web of eternity, fully conscious of every movement around me.

At that point of time and space I was not afraid of Death any longer...

Ama taught me Love braking my boundaries and ego structures to carefully rebuild what was left of me and prepare me for the merge.

The dance we danced that night was called the Dance of Life, together we touched the centre of the circle of existence, following the wheel of destiny, entering the spiral we activated the magic that separates us mortals from Angels, Gods and Spirits.

Lapis that was, the sacred stone that transforms metals into gold, transferring us from the semi-conscious states of mortals into dimensions of meditations, into the Light of the Golden Flower, and powerful energies of Tao transformation. Kundalini awakening, they call it, her velvet skin and Earth Goddess within her eyes took me in.

Broken into millions of pieces, I was the journey from a single drop into the ocean and back into the drop again. That evening when we met in the gardens of her coffee-shop I told her:

"Before I met you I could not imagine non-existence. It was beyond me to comprehend that 'I' in any form of consciousness could cease to exist. To die and awake to be reborn again."

"Are you leaving me?"

Holding her I felt her shiver. Fragile, delicate, brittle, this woman in my arms was, afraid to lose me, and I wanted her to stop me, wanted her to direct me into her eternal embrace. But I feared this will not happen, I feared she will let me walk away, she will let me fly in whichever direction I chose to, even if the direction meant losing me.

If you choose me, we could transform metals into gold together within every Soul we touch. We could prove that it is possible to live Love even with all the obstacles that this choice demands.

The world of Love opened its doors to you, Ama said, and you were privileged to enter. Will you now abandon it all?

Whoever enters knows how difficult it is to get in, but once you are in, you are treated as an honourable guest. Love gives you powers, powers to foresee future, understand past, heal or materialise things. It takes courage to enter the door of knowledge, it takes double to choose to live it. Carrying the responsibility of such a Divine gift might be too heavy to bare.

The ducks across the stream were staring at me with their radiant colours, joyfully playing with the water, competing for the attention of their mates. God's creation in all different forms laughed at me.

The yellow fields of flowers took me to my childhood memories of my mother who I hardly had a chance to meet, she died when I was four. The flowers' yellow gave me a mix of peace and melancholy, a mix of memories with no proper trace or recognition.

My happiness was firmly ground within this material world, its eternal playful game and no doubt I was attached to its allure.

The grass teaches me eternity, teaching me rules of Life's simplicity, born to die, disappear vanish within the chambers of Death to be reborn again from ashes hidden within the Earth.

From a perspective of a Jesuit priest who has a path to follow, God to guide him, and converts to listen to him, it was difficult to admit that I rooted myself deep within grounds of habits, desires and selfishness, just living a dream, walking a path that was still very far from God.

Helping to save poor unbelievers. I separated people to us and them, the more I labelled them as Christians, Buddhists, Atheists, Pagans, the more I suck strength from the body of Christ that lived within me, the more I poisoned my thoughts, killing Life within me.

Entering the Church's embrace, what seduced me most was not the power or the money, Jesuits bow not to ask for money and they live life of ascetics through their journey to God, I was seduced by knowledge that opened its chambers to me. The chamber of knowledge was full of toys and different goods, it was interesting, bewildering, amusing, it kept me occupied for hours, days, years, decades, and it probably could have kept me there a whole lifetime.

Many devils slept in this abode hidden behind veils of superiority, control, arrogance and self-importance. And I remembered that night...

"A bad thought will increase in power and it will overcome you before you realise the darkness of the monstrosity that is approaching behind your back. Use your Will to focus your Mind onto clear judgments, exercise virtues, exercising right thinking, and right living. This effort will help you enter the chamber of knowledge." Ama turned to one of the people within the room, took his hand with the most gentleness telling him that she feels that he managed to work with this quality very powerfully, and that she would like all of us to learn from him and discover the pattern that exists within his Will.

Now, this odd person living in Ama's household, was a rough self-educated Dutch-man, who appeared from nowhere and stayed with them for God knows what reasons. He was a solder, strong, handsome, most of the time silent and withdrawn within his dark misty world. His eyes if you ever had a chance to look at his eyes spelled trouble, his movements were harsh, and he had no name, Ama called him: 'Krishna', 'Milarepa', 'Eagle', 'Iskon', 'Ozon', 'Aron' whatever he wished at the time. When she introduced him, she told us he was her angel and I was jealous of the connection that existed between the two.

Leaving Ama that evening, I was haunted by the obscurity of her choice. What a scavenger's look, no family to call his own, but, what bordered me most, what I could not forget, forgive, or forsake, was a feeling, an inkling, an insight that he might one day become her lover, once upon who knows what time, within who knows what lifetime, now or perhaps in many years down the future, That was undeniable.

My thoughts piled with an astonishing speed and very soon, I was angry and exhausted by all the possibilities, the games my Mind played on me were endless. Soon I hated the poor man who Ama mentioned that fatal night. It took me a night of not sleeping, a night of a sound dreamless sleep and a day of making love, talking and walking with Ama to realise that my Mind had a mortal kiss with the Lady Jealousy, creating a whirlpool of negative emotions that could have been very damaging for all of us. I was humbled by this experience.

It is said that angels start singing once you tell the truth to yourself and people around you, I could not hear mine: a Jesuit, a preacher, a priest, a Portuguese in Macao, a man at the beginning of his journey. Has decided to break the chains of his attachments, all of them!

Father Benedict, a middle aged, greyed hair man, with blue eyes, full of fire, deepened by the many months spent in the company of the vast sea, howling winds, and silence, full of wisdom gained by the many moons of prayer and meditation, in an attempt to understand people and their relationship to God made Ama's vision his own mission fighting for the merge of many to One.

I could have helped Ottavio and father Schall reform the Calendar, translate books, become a part of their task to change the World, Humanity, Religions, Life on Earth.

Through my life, I followed the guidelines from my spiritual teachers vigorously, following superiors, or the Pope, following Ama... I knew of a Jesuit priest who behaved the way the Church wanted him to, I knew a leader, a confessor who led his flock through the difficult times, being what his students wanted him to be, I knew of a man who wanted to be a friend, a soul mate, a lover, a man who knew nothing but what his long awaited newly discovered wife, Ama wanted him to be. But I did not know how to Be.

Awake in the middle of the night, walking through the woods, I prayed...

Wanting to stop the wheel of fortune turning, I wanted to get out of my skin, get out of the Monastery, jump off this voyage on Earth. Perhaps, I did believe in suffering, perhaps the world of happiness, love, togetherness was not just as yet mine. Jesus suffered for the humanity, perhaps, my pain was meant to give strength to the rest of the world?

Fighting against the common enemy, against the Dutch, standing shoulder to shoulder facing Death, with a common goal, was easy; defending Ama against the attacks of my superiors, short minded priests and suspicious citizens of Macao who called Her a witch, our relationship 'blasphemy' was easy, now, I needed to fight against myself, against my deep need to refuse happiness and accept suffering as the way of being!

I will pray for you, were her last words.

And I walked away...

> The Tao that can be told is not the eternal Tao.
> The name that can be named is not the eternal name.
> **Lao Tze Tung**

Ama's Mother

I was born in Kenya, in the tribe that is today known as Pokot. The Pokot people of Kenya belong to the 'Kalenjin' group. People from the tribe are tall and beautiful, very fit and strong and they take pride in their good looks. Today, the people from my tribe are renowned to be very good athletes and very often they win the hardest of races.

As a daughter of a tribal chief I was initiated into secrets of magic and sacred life from an early age and as soon as I reached maturity, I gained the status of Medicine Woman of my Tribe.

In Africa Gods and people live together all the time.

God is everywhere and Nature is God's supreme manifestation. Sun and Moon are His eyes.

God is present with us at all major events: at the birth of our children, circumcision, at our weddings, funerals and at the harvest times. We worship Him every day through our rituals, music, singing and dance.

Before we put any crops into Earth, we sacrifice a cock or a hen or a goat to a God of lands, to a God of crops, or to our ancestors whose spirits protect us from Death.

We create shrines around sacred trees as sanctuaries for animals, humans and prayer temples, a Snake is not called by its name so not to remind her of her powers, and people respect the darkness and its secrets.

The elders of the village taught me how to heal the sick, make sacrifices and pray to Gods for health, rain or victory when my tribe was in a war.

Her Majesty Moon became my protector and was for a long time my best friend. Looking at the moon, night after night, after night, opened my Soul to Her Wisdom.

She taught me about Her different phases and Her influence on Earth. She thought me that we should plant and sow during Her journey from the new to the full and to gather fruit, cut flowers, prune trees during Her journey back to the new moon.

Even the smallest living creatures, ants, are affected by Her powers, they rest and worship Her in their nests when the Moon is new.

She helped me predict weather becoming red as gold when wind is coming, observing Her, I learned when is the best time for bleeding, preparing medicine, baths, or purges.

She has also guided me through all my spiritual discoveries.

When She was descending, disappearing, losing Her powers, I learned to be humble and patient. Following the wisdom of waters I withdrew during the nights of no moon, keeping quiet and still, waiting for the time of activity. When She returned, in Her full glory, illuminating the starry nights She would again teach me expressiveness and beauty of movements and sounds.

All creatures of the savannahs followed this secret dance, so the nights of Her Majesty were very noisy, alive and vibrant. Piercing sounds of frogs, hoppers, locusts and other insects would prevent us from sleep and I would often go down to the lake to admire Her reflection and Her full and magnificent glory.

My ancestors thought me how to fight the sickness, and please the Gods, She thought me how vast the Universe is, and how amazing the laws of our worlds are.

The spirits are beings that live in the world between men and Gods, they are humans that have died and who stayed to help us communicate with Gods. To pass their messages, they appeared in my dreams or I would call them using a special dance or drumming, inviting them to possess me so that they may speak through me while I am in trance. Spirits can act maliciously or with good intentions. I learned how to distinguish the two.

If a man or a woman dies violently or is thrown away without a burial, they might return as evil spirits hungry for revenge. They can possess men and cause illnesses such as madness or fever or may endanger a village through an outbreak of epidemics. These must be driven away. My task was to convince them to leave.

As Medicine Woman and the second to the village priestess, I was sometimes called to help the village rain-maker to call or dismiss the rain. When the elements became too heavy and persistent, or in the heart of the very dry season, when even the rain maker's efforts became futile, I would help him so that extremes of weather do not hurt him in his attempts to interfere.

In harvest times, I was involved in the village feast, giving thanks to the Earth Goddess, the source of all fertility and to the ancestral spirits of the clan, who will oversee the harvest, bless it and ensure a fruitful season, a season of plenty.

Some months before the Portuguese landed with their ships and soldiers, I had a dream about their arrival.

The wise man and elders met and discussed dreams: the arrival of a white man was to be bloody and full of suffering but was not to be for long and was to lead to the spread of our people and culture into the new worlds and new continents. It looked as though God had a plan for us and a plan was in our defeat. There was no other choice but to follow.

During the 16th century my father's tribe was defeated and I knew that my destiny was far away on the shores of new lands. I was taken away from Kenya as a slave.

I managed to find a protector in a man who I saved from Death using herbs that I brought with me. Fear or gratitude made him take care of me until we reached the Portuguese lands. There, I made my presence known to Ottavio De Nobille, a Portuguese magician and a priest who could read dreams and communicate with spirits. He recognised me and came to my rescue, he bought me and made me his companion, his wife, his teacher and seven years later, the mother of his daughter Ama.

Our marriage, our Alchemical Marriage, was a marriage of a powerful spiritual man, the white king within Portuguese Worlds and me, the queen of magic and mysteries, his black queen.

Together, our knowledge multiplied hundreds of times. Together, our souls were reborn and we undertook the alchemical process of transmutation.

I thought him the power of herbs, and stones and metals, and the way to access their spirits to heal all sort of diseases.

"With the magic we can increase our bodily powers, suggest foods for a particular disease, strengthen the vital energies with tools like music, colours, or scents, but we still stay mortal, weak humans that oscillate and change with a simple change of temperature, pressure, or chemicals within our brain," he insisted.

"To find the secret of true happiness or immortality we need to go a step further, we need to learn the secret of creation. If we can gain spiritual strength to change ordinary consciousness into the pure awareness, we can hope to share the reality of starry worlds and become immortal."

Ottavio did sometimes publicly display some of his magic powers.

Once he helped the authorities find the murderer of the villager whose body was found in the woods. Three people were under the suspicion. He advised the council to bring the suspects to the fresh corpse knowing that the body will start bleeding from the wound in the presence of the murder. As though, the dead victim felt the presence of the killer and got again agitated by anger and fear, the miracle did happen, the wound started bleeding again when the third man walked passed it. Scared by the event, the murderer admitted the charges.

Anyway, Ottavio said to the police that was still amazed with the result, even a magician of a very limited understanding should know this little secret kept within the body of the murdered, the knowledge of the murderer.

Both Alchemy and Magic are sciences explaining secret side of God's laboratory. The fact that we hide them, code and mystify their words and processes is also a part of God's plan.

Ottavio's spirit, had within itself a mighty fire, he was strong and analytical, very different from mine that was connected to Her Majesty the Moon, was female in every sense of the word. His strength and my surrender gave a birth to the Perfection, to Gold, to our daughter Ama.

When she was born I died to became a living-dead following her throughout her life, protecting her and guiding her through her youth, until she was 35 when she was ready to move through Earth alone.

That evening, at Ole, in Macao, at the tip of China, on the planet Earth, my daughter Ama was narrating a story. The colour of her skin, in a weird way, has protected her from the well-sealed destiny of a woman of her age. If Ama was born white she would have probably been married and kept in a golden cage of a family life within many prejudices of a man's society, but born black and born of a slave mother, God gave her an unusual freedom and a possibility to live whatever she wanted.

That evening Ama was sitting surrounded with people of all ages and they were all in a way her followers, admirers, and students. It was late and logs of disappearing fire in the centre of the gathering were radiating a red hue. The smell of burning wood was in the air, the sky was clear and illuminated by bright stars and the magic of the spring was enchanting the crowds.

The atmosphere was one of a serene calmness, peace and surrender to the expectation of a promise.

Ama said that tonight she will tell us a story, a story about a lost land and a lost civilisation that lived on Earth thousands of years ago. She said that this story is important to understand where we came from, and where we, as humankind, are heading.

An echo of someone's thought or just a breath of wonder caught in between two moments was the only sound that managed to escape the block of silence that formed when Ama was story-telling.

'Long before the human race as we know it today, long before the Chinese, Spanish or Portuguese empire, long before Buddha, Christ, Romans, Egyptians or Greeks, an island with unparalleled beauty was the home of a race that called itself 'Sons of Gods'. The place was called: 'Centre where the Will of God is known'.

In China this civilisation is known as Sons of Reflected Light, and in Egypt as Companions of Horus. It is believed that they brought their knowledge to us from across the sea.

Legend has it that this place was ruled by Enlightened Kings guarding the highest Wisdom ever obtained.

Sons of Gods had beautiful, long, strong bodies, faces with high foreheads, sharp noses and strong black eyebrows. Tall and lean, subtle, and mysterious, they understood Tao. Their eyes carried amazing beauty coloured yellowish, brownish, green, a colour that reminds one of a leaf during early Autumn days.

The weather of this magical place was quite extraordinary. There were no distinct seasons or maybe it is better to say, at all times of the year, there were all seasons present. The seasons coexisted in harmony with each other.

They passed to us the knowledge of how to make glass and pottery, how to use metals and medicine, how to work with silk and make art, and to the few, they also passed the secrets of Spirit.

They spent most of their time experimenting, exploring, researching different ways of living with others on the Planet.

They saw Earth as an animated being that within its delicate net hides the spirits that influence all.

Instead of building houses to protect them from rain, wind and snow as we do today, they lived in harmony with elements, in harmony with Nature. They were able to send signals and messages to other beings throughout the Universe.

They learnt from Nature to foretell the future and to understand the past. They knew the inner virtues of sun, planets, vegetables, minerals, and animals, what qualities are latent within them; what is their purpose, and their properties, and what their occult possibilities are. Knowing the secrets of Nature they attempted to know God.

They also became masters of their dream states. For them sleeping was just a continuation of the Work on the Self.

For them every thought and sound carried a meaning and strength of materialisation.

They mastered formulas and sounds that could materialise forms and their sacred rituals were based on these, they have never wasted their precious time and energy on interactions that would not inspire them or teach them something new.

But as it is on Earth, all that has its beginning, has its end, this race also approached its-own end.

The children were playing near the woods and were waiting for their teacher to appear and in their innocence they 'interfered'.

'Why did you stop the rain!'

the Wise One shouted when He arrived. It was rare to see him shout, it was rare to see him upset, but this event changed the history of the race.

'Who gave you the right to interfere!'

Anticipating His lecture they've decided to interfere. It was not difficult to stop the rain. If the mind is focussed, even a child's mind can do it, clouds will listen, the wind will listen and the rain will go away. A ritual lasted a few minutes and children saw the black clouds withdraw and the storms disappear.

The little play was even amusing and powers performed were seductive but he wasn't amused.

'I do not want to follow your individual wills.
I want to participate in His flow.
And if He sends the rain, there is a good reason for it.
How can you believe that your minds know better than Him?
What if you have just disturbed a number of happenings that would have occurred with this rain?

And what if the rain would have brought us experiences that are much stronger than the ones that we are expecting now?

You did not trust Him!

You were not attentive enough to the sounds of forest and Earth's joyful murmurs for rain and with your selfishness you have transformed them into a cry.

I've heard this cry coming to meet you and it is haunting me at this moment!

As it was predicted, the incidences kept occurring.

The predictions were becoming their reality, the predictions about the end of their journey and the split that will happen amongst them, the split that will allow them to pass the knowledge, when the time is right, in a different way, to the future generation to come.

The Wise Men already knew the decision. After some meditation and experiments with the knowledge of the past, present and future, they announced the best way forward.

They split Sons of God into three groups.

One of the groups was transferred to an isolated island. To protect the island from outside forces, visitors and curious or evil spirits, the chiefs cut it off using mountain ranges, deep waters and vast lands. To reach it, one would need to descend into the depths of Earth, following the path of red hot lava; or climb the highest mountains surrounded by ice and meters of snow into the areas from where no man has ever returned. The mission of this group is to stay on Earth and continue influencing the major energies of the Supreme Mother Gaya's matrix. They are not to be met by Men and their presence is not to be known.

The second group transformed into tree Devas: tree spirits that inhabit trees that are able to live thousands of years. Their bodies merged with the ones of trees that outlived most civilisations, wisely observing their passage through time. The Hindus recognised the hidden powers of these Beings and they worshiped the old trees, the Chinese kept large forests untouched as their temples, the Egyptians knew that they were divine. Many spiritual disciples sat beneath the branches of old trees to strengthen their spiritual growth and get the necessary inspiration. We all can still communicate with them but to be able to do so we need to learn the language of Silence.

The third group decided to stay on Earth as spirits, mostly invisible or visible only to a few.

All the ancient cultures talk about this race.

Confucians talk about this age. They talk about the time when the Great Way was practised, when people lived good faith and in affection. The race that did not regard as parents only their own parents, or as sons only their own sons, but that lived in harmony with all, as brothers. This was the age of Great Unity.

The Persians took the custom, never to admit anyone as a king unless he was a Wise Man. The king was to the country a king, a priest, a prophet, a magician, and a scholar of Nature. The Egyptians too, had the knowledge of the secrets of Nature and they also asked from their kings to acquire the wisdom of priests and magicians.

Whether Christians or Buddhist or Taoist, we all seek to find this place at the end of our journeys.

Weaving this amazing matrix of our past, present and future, we connect to Sons of God, and to our perfect life in a different, more enlightened Earth.

All the movements start within our own excellence."

This evening was one of many at Ottavio's coffee and tea house called 'Ole'.

That night, after a séance, Ama faced me with her loving kindness and maturity of an enlightened being and asked me to leave and join higher realms of existence because she was all set to continue her journey without me.

As any mother would I protected my little one the best I could, all through her life on Earth. I guarded her sleep from disturbed spirits when she was a child, I directed the first cannon against the Dutch during the attack to Macao, and the great storm (you will learn about it later) that scared Chinese and led to release of Father Schall was in my hands.

When I died Ottavio helped me through my transition, he spent days and days in prayers guiding my soul. When he died, I was there to guide him, when Ama died, if she has ever died, only Light could be seen in heavens, no trace of attachment just pure Light.

'...as there is no truth which is not joined or opposed to what is false, so there is no love without fear, ardour, jealousy, rancour, and other passions, which proceed from their opposites, and which disturb us, as the other opposite causes satisfaction. Thus the soul striving to recover its natural beauty seeks to purify itself, to heal itself, and to reform itself, and to this end it uses fire, because, being like gold, mixed with earth and crude, with a certain rigour it tries to liberate itself from defilement, and this result is obtained when the intellect, the real smith of love, puts itself to the work and causes an active exercise of the intellectual powers.'

Giordano Bruno

Chronology of a Minor Famine in 17th Century China

The virus that has attacked us was a minor one. Yet who can imagine panic who has not lived through one? We may have known sickness of various forms yet this one came in a burst of many people's thoughts all passed to us through various media. This was a minor virus with a death count not larger than norm...

Who can imagine the panic of a city? The panic of the suburbs, the great sweep of fear and the anxious eyes of the stomach twisting.

Still, they say this famine was a minor one, no more than one of many that struck the humanity so many times before. The temples have closed and the royals did stop the public audiences, and the grand procession was cancelled. The one who died, for the most part, only the aged, or the ones with an underlying condition, a weak heart or a smoky chest, along the ones weakened by other illness or by loss of hope.

Just Before

The market emptied early with the good folk carrying off expensive purchases and the others going off with extra food, safe for another day. Public gatherings and wedding feasts were postponed or cancelled with gold prices rise, for we all know that it is good to purchase gold when the World falls down. Or as someone else has wisely said: Fear and hunger breeds revolution.

"There is a big war coming", said the wise woman observing the spread.

Plump bodies grew bigger, for the lack of moving, and thin ones stronger, for no movement was allowed.

The shops, the owners, the glittering entertainment industry will soon rise above its losses, will recover and grow fat again. Perhaps it is possible for us to imagine a minor panic.

Now this is where our experiences diverge in two, the ones who could and the ones who could not re-fill the empty balls. Some of us have also gone through a minor famine, listening to the wailing of children or a grumpy wife with their stomachs twisting in pain. We might or might not be able to fill that gap, the gap between a earth-quake that has caused the minor famine, in a minor kitchen of a minor few, who have lost their half legal professions or closed their, just managed to open barber shops.

"Now is the right time for the practice of Compassion, do it in steps: remember yourself, exercise, and contemplate." I've heard one of the Moon Ladies on our little Planet alter.

Some time before -

The 7th day of the 7th lunar month is the end of the rainy season in China, the time of harvest, the time of the Night called All Souls Night was the night of the great earth-quake.

Some tales ought to be told and told again, re-vibrating the same truths over and over, for if it's not our flesh to hurt, we think the pain to be just a game in a rehearsal of life.

Some tales ought to be told quickly, as a glance or dance over an ice-coated river, for we, souls incarnated to learn, cannot absorb them into our Being just as yet, for our aura floods with different colours.

Children have deep longing to believe that World is based on Truth and only parents have the true respect for that longing. The orphans in any city will tell you many tales, most of them myths, half-truth, half lies, for it is only the myth that can protect their fragile souls from the colours of the reality. Within their family mythology or constellation they managed to live beyond the ordinary, becoming extra-ordinary... Now, they had no problems imagining a famine, even a small one, run chills up their spines. For each encounter of a man, was the one of disorderly causes and effects by no mean predictable effects.

Extraordinary times call for extraordinary measures.

Riot police clash with market traders.

Traders shouted "The King must go".

Thousands of people thronged the country suffer.

'End of the world'

A powerful earthquake has struck north of China's capital, damaging buildings, burying vehicles in rubble and causing several fires.

The major earthquake strikes all of China.

Prime Minister said the earthquake was the biggest in the last 140 years.

Several fires were also reported. Residents without homes sleep on the squares.

Soldiers wearing masks and carrying shovels could be seen helping efforts to clear the damage on the streets.

The overcrowded housing, a lack of sewage systems, and unsafe drinking water. Government sees "Overcrowding is a huge issue,"

People are relatively isolated, they have inadequate access to healthcare, the housing is after the disaster crowded... food insecurity is an issue and certainly unemployment rates – those all act to make people more vulnerable.

This is a "crisis waiting to happen,"
'God's punishment':

"God told me through his holy book, Quran, to urge people to refrain from sin. Our bad deeds will be punished. The earth-quake is God's punishment," A man surrounded by a small crowd said.

Several states have declared states of emergencies and ordered the closures of businesses.

We have declared a national emergency. The governance has been under fire for all the issues that the country has faced.

The Buddhist Temple is turning into a giant warehouse as a base to store food and other essential items which will be delivered by a team of volunteers.

This is casing the Great Recession.

Earlier this month the Government has released prisoners to help reduce the risk of the diseases spreading in its prisons.

Global hunger could double due to the Earth-quakes all through the countries.

Some residents continue to live in tents more than 18 months after the triple disaster of earth-quake, fire and disease.

In light of the attack from the Invisible Enemy, as well as the need to protect the jobs

This disease has targeted those with the poorest health.

Many moons before in the parallel Universe called Earth...

Li Po was an artist, a painter, my Chinese language teacher, and the guide through the vastness of Chinese culture and the way of thinking. This tiny gentleman was ancient, but very vital and alive with a small white beard, long white hair tied in a ponytail, educated in Peking, and now living in Macao. He had a studio teaching Chinese brushwork.

One of the first major conflicts between the Catholic movement and Chinese authorities occurred during 1616 when a high ranking official in Nanjing, called Shen Huai, advised the Emperor that Catholicism should be banned. The conflicts between Chinese customs like Confucianism and ancestor worship and the Catholic customs like baptism led to the anti-Christian movement. Shen Huai arrested dozens of missionaries for questioning. According to him, Catholicism taught Chinese not to respect parents, or worship ancestors and this was a great sin. Urged by the Anti-Catholic movement, Emperor Wenli passed a law deporting all foreign missionaries back to their homeland.

The conflict about accepting or not accepting Chinese customs, reflected through the conflict about the Christian terminology used in spreading Catholicism in China. Matteo Ricci's approach was to adopt the Confucian practice, referring to God as Tian Zhu: the Ruler of Heaven, or Tian: Heaven. But, after Ricci's death, some of the missionaries believed that these terms cannot represent God and that only Latin terminology should be used.

We, within the Jesuit movement, have understood the delicacy of the matter and we allowed our Chinese converts to continue with ancestor worship. The Augustinians, on the other hand, were not of the same opinion and they banned this most sensible tradition as heresy. This caused us a lot of problems with the Chinese Government.

After a cup of tea, my teacher Li Po was always looking for an excuse to have tea, served in the courtyard of his house, we wondered around his gardens, talking about Chinese Gods and Spirits.

"Chinese culture hosts many different Gods, Spirits, and myths," my Chinese host meditatively introduced the subject of our discourse. "We believe that every living thing is spiritual, that all, wood, stones, animals, are spiritual beings manifested in matter.

We believe that everything is just a countless manifestation of one and the same Chi, spiritual energy.

Everything just reflects its Divine origin: a stick, a house, a blade of grass, earth or a star. Because of its Divine Nature, we give it all its due attention and worship."

In a pursuit of happiness and harmony, the Chinese philosophers carefully studied the mysterious influences of Nature, a bit like my Ancient Greeks and Ancient Egyptians, looking into the stars, observing earth, comparing essences of different elements.

The Chinese were checking the pulses of earth for centuries, to learn how to select an auspicious place or time for an activity. Within this complicated system of knowledge, one can say when the Harmony is achieved or when it is broken.

"For example, should anyone suddenly fall sick, it is almost certain that the Chinese will find its cause in the disturbed energy within the area." Said my host.

"Disagreeing with Tao means suffering, if a man obstruct or disturb a valley, or a river, the insulted element will revenge causing an illness or misfortune."

"Chinese Gods are not always very benevolent," said Li Po smiling, "they sometimes bring suffering. They could be moody, have peculiar personalities and are responsible for calamities, disasters, lack of harmony and unhappiness. We give our respect to all of them, the benevolent ones and the ones that create disorder, and fear."

As in every other country, the Chinese world was divided into the crowds that followed blindly and educated minority that was defining the moral code. The hundreds of fortune teller and roadside oracles that I saw on the marketplace, and in the streets of Chinese towns, were mainly an entertainment for masses.

"The book at the very core of the early Chinese philosophical thought, serving as a common ground for the Confucian and Taoist, is called Yi Jing," my host said bringing forth a book that we studied in the years to come.

It was an early edition, a true work of art, composed by famous calligraphers.

Confucius wrote a commentary for this book, around 500 BC, and his wise words became the conduct code of the Chinese Kings and society.

"We believe that spirit and matter are two aspects of the same thing. Spirit is inherent in matter. We also believe that **change** is inherent in the cosmic order."

The original meaning of 易 yi is the lizard, that changes its color according to its place, and it is a combined character of the sun 日 (Yang) and the moon 月 (Yin); Yì has 3 meanings: **Simplicity** - the fundamental law underlying everything in the universe is simplicity; **Change** - the universe is continually changing; and **Persistency** - a central rule that does not fluctuate with space and time. 經 Jīng means sutra, scripture, or a great teaching.

The Yi Jing reflects the universe in miniature. Each picture, each hexagram, illustrates one aspect of 'Chi' and the subtle Yin-Yang interaction that exist in nature.

The hexagram consists of a solid (Yang) and a broken (Yin) line, and signifies the change between Yang and Yin. The book consists of 64 hexagrams, or combinations of the solid and broken line. Each hexagram looks at life from a different angle and all together they cover all aspects of life. This grid of polarities spans the spectrum from Yin to Yang, describing the relationships between the two opposites.

Everything in Nature manifests either through Heavenly Father or through Mother Earth. Yang is strong, muscular, pure, and vigorous and Yin is gentle, feminine, flexible, fertile and patient. Yin gives and maintains life.

Balance is achieved only when Yin and Yang are in harmony.

To help me further understand the concept of Yin and Yang, that is so deeply engrained within Chinese way of thinking, my teacher opened the book and guided my focus onto two hexagrams that form the basis of the Yi Jing philosophy. The Yi Jing starts with the hexagrams Qian and Kun. Qian is heaven and Kun is earth. When heaven and earth are born; the whole of creation comes into being.

My mind wondered for my research got me into the possession of a George Ripley Alchemical manuscripts. He was a sovereign in Yorkshire living from 1415 to 1495. The Alchemist George Ripley was in a pursuit of the Philosophers' Stone.

Excuse my luck of focus but satisfying yours forever thirsty curiosity, this story travels through the channels of Cam, ascends the hills of Edinburgh and enters Oxford's castles, exploring very rare manuscript that use both verses and images to portray ancient esoteric teachings.

For all the mystical researchers, the copy I researched 'Hermes Trismegistus' was drawn during my time, during the 16th century. Dozens of alchemical drawings accompany Ripley's poems "Verses upon the Elixir", "Boast of Mercury", "Trinity". These images pass the message of our hermaphrodite Universe, of Kundalini awakening, of Life going forth seeking to materialize in all possible forms, of the sacred movement towards perfection. Meditating on the images entering a journey of encountering various mythological creatures, we are shown a processes for the production of the philosopher's stone in pictorial cryptograms.
Now this Ripley's Scroll shows 7 stages of transformation, an egg shaped vase grey in color, possible of becoming any shape, color or form, full of sperm like tadpole released by a huge green frog

presumably in water, as eggs that hatch and through its growth develop limbs and lungs undergoing the most amazing metamorphosis.

Eight of the mandalas, seven depicting alchemical experiments; while the eight is a Biblical scene of Adam and Eve and Tree of Knowledge. The scroll continues exploring the story of Adam and Eve, they stand in water surrounded by 7 alchemists with their transformational processes. At the top of the tree of knowledge is a naked dragon tailed woman with "Speritu" encrypted on her, holding a child with "Anima" hanging from the branches caressing the naked boy; followed by Adam with a sign of Sun and Eve who worships Moon, standing beside the Tree of Knowledge, observed by the serpent and alchemists.

This scene is in the center of Sun and Moon, facing each other, each with feathers, totally reminded me of the Chinese Yin and Yang.

The original meaning of Qian is the brilliant sunshine at sunrise. It inspires all life, making it prosperous. The hexagram Qian has six masculine and solid lines. Its symbol is the dragon. The dragon is a sacred animal; it represents the prestige of the king. It is dynamic as the power of Nature; it is comfortable both in water and in the sky.

Qian is in an essence of creativity, benevolence and righteousness.

The image of Kun is earth. It is pure femininity. Earth creates the world and nourishes it. The whole of creation counts on it for nurture and growth. Kun is a female horse. The horse galloping without limits, to the horizon; with tenderness and submissiveness as its main quality.

"This book never fails to grant us access to eternity." Contemplated Li Po.

And how exactly does it work? I wondered.

"We follow a meditation ritual to calm our mind and gain an access to our inner self. We focus on the relevant issue, ask a question or guideline from the book, and its answer inspires our intuition to define correct course of action."

"Does that mean that the answer is already within us?" I asked.

"Correct," he confirmed!

"That means that we could be using any book?"

He smiled. "Nearly all the greatest minds of China used this book or have written an interpretation of its text," he said avoiding the direct answer, "the wisdom of thousands of years is within the Yi Jing. Why would you seek another book?"

"Correct," I smiled...

"Talking about ceremonies!" He exclaimed! "Please now do join me for my tea ceremony!"

We spent lots of time in his studio, a clean, uncluttered and peaceful place that inspired my friend's work. The studio had a large desk full of ink-stones, rolls of paper, some finished and unfinished paintings, bamboo brushes and beautifully carved holders. The colour dishes and a fresh flower floating in one of the water bowls regularly acknowledged my presence.

Li Po was famous for his calligraphy, the art of drawing Chinese characters.

It took me time and patience to convince him to teach me calligraphy 'cause his artist mind saw this quazi-effort of mine as a waste of time. Teaching a foreigner, a Westerner, who is expecting to learn something about this sacred art in less than a life-time was silly. But he finally gave up his fight and opened for me a little paradise into the art of this ancient science. Carefully observing my friend and teacher paint in front of me, I would observe his strokes, his movements, his compositions, and what he wanted me to get from this observation were his feelings, moods, states of mind.

"Each character is a living entity, with its own energy and the force that awakens within the drawing of the symbol.

Each sentence is a poem, a meditation, a prayer, a combination of characters that cannot be taken lightly."

He drew only extracts from sacred texts. When the lesson was over, I would take his paintings home, study them, copy them for hours, and bring them back the next day for his criticism.

Copying characters over and over again, I learned the symbols, techniques, the use of colours, the way to hold the brush, but also, I was immersing my Soul into the subconscious wisdom of each symbol, delivering my intellect to the higher intuitive force that lived within the characters for millions of years.

As you might already know, there is no such thing as an alphabet in Chinese. A character or symbol is more than a letter or a word, it is a concept and behind it there are sometimes many words.

Originally, thousands years ago, each character was a small picture, but now these are simplified keeping the essence of each drawing.

"For the most basic use, and for reading the scripts, you need to master about 3,000 characters," my teacher said, with the look of amusement in his eyes.

"So how many do you know?"

"More than 30,000!" He laughed, leaving me with amusing wonderment about the numbers mentioned...

"We begin writing at the top of a page, on the right-hand side and we continue writing vertically. We also open our books from the side you consider to be the back side of the book."

"Speech and writing," Li Po explained, "both express the same impulse, conveyance of thought, one through hearing, other through sight. Speech is followed by the music of words, while the writing is there to liberate the beauty of symbols. The art of character writing is very sacred in China."

There is a definitely defined order to strokes, from left to right and from top to bottom, an order in which a symbol is enclosed within the other.

"Learning to draw Chinese characters," my teacher continued, "the most important is that 'Chi Yün' enters your heart. Chi Yün is spirit-vitality or life-breath of a painting. It is intangible but unless it is born within your heart, you can copy the characters all your life and you still will not draw them correctly."

A relationship between Chinese and symbols is very profound.

"I've heard that some Daoist painters paint with their hair achieving 'wild' curves and 'spontaneous' effects." I asked.

"For example, look at this reproduction of Wang Xizhi's famous work: The Introduction to the Orchid Pavilion, how beautiful, original, spontaneous, and rhythmic it is! Wang Xizhi lived around 300 AC and he is was a Chinese Sage of Calligraphy. All through China his calligraphy is carefully collected and studied. This book was written during one poetry contest. He was a Governor and he invited forty artists to this contest. After the event, he wrote the preface to accompany the poems within the book." Li Po was fascinated by this Sage,

What fascinated me more within this little story is the poetry contest that happened almost two thousand years ago. They gathered to write about Life, to philosophy, to share their deeper insights two thousand years ago, 300 years before Christ was born!

Somehow, my mind could not grasp the thought of thousands of years in the past. Yet it has happened and it has been recorded, we did exist, they shout from their graves and we wrote poetry, drew characters, sat next to the streams, laughing, drinking, exchanging, and then publishing it, for future generations, for posterity, showing teeth to mortality and its deadly bite of 'forgetness'.

"The oldest found records are our Oracle bone scripts," my teacher was explaining, "symbols were first written with a brush, and then inscribed with an animal bone tool."

I could imagine that a lot of original calligraphy did not survive because it was drawn on very fragile silk or paper. The ones that survived were mostly inscribed in stone or bamboo.

Li Po showed me a page bound together of bamboo sticks that all had vertical inscription looking like columns.

"Important religious texts like the Buddhist sutras were engraved on the bamboos, or rock faces of sacred mountains." He said.

"Like the one done on Mount Tai." I remembered seeing this little interaction of people of our past and Nature.

"Yes, during those days, the copies of the entire Buddhist canon were commissioned by the Emperor. The most talented calligraphers did the work."

"It is a great honour for a calligrapher to be asked to do the scrolls, it is a sign of respect of the artist's potential."

Calligraphy has remained a potent force in Chinese life up to the present days. I studied the language, the symbols, the myths, because I wanted an insight into China's visual culture, into their customs, into their beliefs, for I was a scientist, not only to devise my-own methods in converting Chinese into Christianity.

As a mean of the visual communication, Chinese characters are fascinating in their ingenuity, portraying the philosophical idea behind the word.

For example, 'xin' is a character for heart and mind. Chinese see heart and mind as one and the same thing.

The frame or state of mind comes from the heart, not from the head as you are accustomed to. A personal insight also uses 'xin' as its main character.

A symbol 'zheng' is an ideograph of a foot walking in a straight line. It also signifies arrival at the line (which is a proper limit) without going astray. The symbol could be translated as: straight, upright, correct, exact and it is used in words such as: normal, proper, rightful, decent, official, justice, etc.

'Jian' is drawn as two spears shattering and destroying the value of shells, and it conveys the idea of cheap, worthless, mean, things that are of little value, but it is also used to depict a poor and miserable person.

"How do you say 'beautiful'," I asked Li Po what I thought was a simple question during one of the lessons?

He stayed quiet for a moment, pensive and amused of the differences that exist between our two worlds, our two languages, our two ways of thinking.

"There are many types of 'beautiful', beautiful as a flower, beautiful as a woman, beautiful within an art object, and so on. Word 'beautiful' does not properly define the concept of beauty that is so vast and deep as an ocean. That is why in our language we use different ways to express all these types of beauty. We do not search for 'fast' solutions and simplify such a magnificent notion such as 'beauty'. We give it a meaning, word, symbol related to the object that carries the beauty."

The world of symbols doesn't live alone. It is interwoven with signs, imagination, superstitions, magic, and dreams. At the beginning of my stay in Macao, I went to a Chinese friend all set to make a good impression with a gift for my host, five packs of a precious and expensive black tea. The gift was taken with whispers, giggles and stares. The host and his wife were amused with the confusion that followed. They explained that the same word 'wu' that is used to indicate the number five, is also used to indicate evil, black, unhappy, violent, militant and that it is a sign of disrespect to give five items as a gift. The inauspicious omen was taken lightly just because I was a foreigner.

A lucky direction brings success while the unlucky one helps the rivals. I could see how much practical trouble this would give to set-up an important business meeting. For what is 'lucky' for one is not necessarily 'lucky' for the other businessman and one can go to an indefinite postponement of the meeting if the two omens never meet.

"On hearing a crow," Li Po continued, "I could tell you your future. If coming from the South in the early morning, you will receive a present, if heard mid-morning there will be rain, if at midday, you will quarrel, if in the afternoon, you will have a misfortune and if you hear it in the evening, you will face a lawsuit."

My face couldn't hide an expression of a complete unbeliever, Li Po smiled:

"This must sound like a lot of gibberish to your mind. However, the Nature continuously presents us with signs. Your point about our free-will is true. Personally I hear the signs but I don't let them rule my life unless there is an important happening, such as building a new home, or choosing a wedding day for your beloved children. Building a home we obey rituals that take care of the direction of the main door, the time of the year, favourite and disturbing winds, trees and house surroundings. The lucky day will lead to reach descendants, to finding a hidden treasure or a promotion to higher office."

Many believe that if an unlucky day or unfavourable place is chosen for a burial, this might lead to calamities and epidemics in the family for years after the funeral. This belief led to quite an abuse by many so-called experts that determine the luckiest date or the luckiest place for a reward. You can imagine people refusing to bury their loved ones in fear that they do not get it right. Government had to stop this motion, because of the disease that spread from such places, and the chaos that was created in an attempt to ensure the best burial places...

"Many found the way to abuse the superstitious, earning their fortune on the misfortune and stupidity of others. But fools are universal, they can be found in all of countries..."

This mixture of what my mind called: superstitious gibberish and the serenity of my host passed shiver through my spine. I did not want to argue or frighten my host, such a gentle and honest person, I humbly took the role of a student, listening attentively and absorbing his words.

"This amazing mix of values gave birth to Chinese Christians whose beliefs are quite a bizarre mix, don't you think?" I asked Li Po a question that was on my mind for some time.

"You will have no problems converting the Chinese into Christians, as long as we could also worship other Gods. Is that acceptable to you? Christ is welcomed into our houses if it is surrounded with the God of Fertility, God of Death, and God of Harvest. If there is to be any success in the conversion to Christianity, you have to let Chinese Christians continue with their ancestor worships." I felt that Li Po was right.

Staying faithful to One God, we, Church Officials, have announced all Chinese Gods non-existent, a culture that was so connected to worship was declared as the culture of non-believers.

"This is indeed a cause of many debates between the missionaries in China." I told Li Po

"You have a strong reputation in Europe and here in China, for your knowledge of astrology, astronomy and mathematics and this reputation could become your strongest weapon. Some of the manuscripts that you have written and translated have reached and impressed the Court. The educated classes of China will listen to your words with respect." Li Po naturally bowed while talking about my work at University.

Living in Macao, on the crossroad of eras, walking from the Dark Ages to the Ages of Science, I was creating a bridge between the two systems of science and religious thoughts, both carrying within the wisdom of their ancestors. My mission became to make them available to anybody who had ears to hear and eyes to see.

"There are many paths leading to One." This time I was with Ama, walking, talking and collecting herbs in the fields of Macao. "These herbs carry within their fragile essence a secret of Life, Universe, Creation."

Walking and talking with this young lady, I remembered the story Ottavio told me about her birth.

Ama's mother was an African princess Ottavio was madly in love with. Brought from Africa as a slave, he bought her, gave her freedom, and married her when she was still very young. They lived together for 7 years childless and she stayed pregnant on their journey to Asia. Ama's mother died minutes after Ama was born. Ottavio believed that she has sacrificed her life for the birth of this special Soul.

Ottavio used to recall that before the day the ship first time touched Macao he had a dream of an angel wounding him with a spear. Blood from the wound got mixed with the mud of Earth that has opened beneath him and a most amazing flower was born from the depths of the darkness that gazed at him. The voice that whispered from the darkness was murmuring 'Life for Life without boundaries'.

His wife understood the dream to be prophesy of a birth of a child of his blood that will grow to be an extraordinary spiritual being.

He took Ama under his protection and educated her in the best possible way. She spoke Swahili, her mother's tongue, Portuguese, the tongue of her father, and Chinese, the tongue of the country she was born in.

Familiar with philosophy, different religious systems, art, mathematics, chemistry, biology, physics, it was always a pleasure talking to her. She was Ottavio's pride and his life experiment, and with every year that passed, she was transforming into a more and more precious flower.

Ama was the only one Ottavio would unconditionally listen to. Her calmness and warmth and his complete trust in her wisdom, created a bond that was visible every time the two were together.

"As a priest and a Christian," I told Ama, "I deeply believe that the vast knowledge hidden within the various religious scripts springs from One Source. No matter how good a religion is, its institution and its rules, ultimately degenerate, bringing stagnation, prejudices, and misunderstandings."

Within Macao, I found a fertile ground for mixing ideas, intentions and dreams of both Chinese and Europeans.

Very early on, I realised that European astronomy and astrology advanced in a different direction to Chinese and that the knowledge of European astronomy could benefit Chinese in building their Annual Calendar.

It was a late summer evening and the coffee shop was closed for public. In the centre of the hall was the fountain and we could hear the water flow intermingle with our breathing. Windows were opened inviting the smell of the Ocean to join the smoke of the Nag Jampa. The wind was playing with chimes, and the low light of candles created a dance of shadows on the floor and on the wall in front of us.

"Respecting the knowledge of our Ancestors, Saints and Scientists, applying Clear Reason and Intuitive Wisdom within this dynamic orphic, hermaphrodite Universe of Unconscious mind Manifestations, at this stage of our evolution, we ask own Souls: how to live life healthier, happier, or stronger.." Said Ama.

"When public libraries appeared, books were often chained to a bookshelf or a desk to prevent theft. As you can imagine it was not book lovers who would ever steal, for how many book lovers were poor or uneducated? Jews didn't quite have public libraries where a "stranger" could possibly hope to learn Hebrew and explore the script within their local knowledge set-up. Judaism values the Torah scroll to such an extent that if placed in a synagogue it must be written by hand on parchment so a printed book would not do." Ama was thinking aloud.

"In the Islamic Golden Age, 8th century to 13th, Islamic calligraphy, miniatures and bookbinding flourished, yet none of the images within the books had any religious connotations. Yaqubi 9th century, says that in his time Baghdad had over a hundred booksellers. Today we find the most beautiful poems exploring God – Allah, yet the illustrations are very generic: flowers, or simple decorations. Within Islam we find no images of Christ or Allah, so no idol worship could take place. Listening to our historians, we know for certain that the destroyed books, and art works are irreplaceable, often changing history in various ways. Being too busy arguing various points of views, philosophizing, or fighting own partner, we assume that somewhere else animals do not need rearing, plants watering, sick do not need care, and children fall perfect from the sky. Within this life-long quest, so many of us create our-own little Universes, marrying and building own "perfect" families, yet the reflection inside the life-mirror says over and over that we err, especially when expressing judgments too hasty..." Ama continued with her meditations.

"Examining the tree, its bark and its root, we miss the picture of the forest and its organic growth."

"One is a female approach," said Ottavio, "intuitive and dreamy, while the other is a male, scientific, precise and clear."

For many centuries the scientific thought was blocked, channelled into the dark corridors of dogmas, that now, when it was released, I still feared, that the critical mass to move the change might not happen.

Throughout the history of what we call "ancient Rome", the Greek was spoken by the well-educated elite, who acquired Greek tutors from educated Greek prisoners, slaves. Within the Byzantine Empire, that was mine home-town, the books were rare and often forbidden.

China led the books printing revolution. The first completed printed book on paper is the Diamond Sutra during the ninth century. Around 1040, the first known movable type porcelain printing press was created in China by Bi Sheng. The copper movable type printing originated in China at the beginning of the 12th century. It was used in large-scale printing of paper money issued by the Northern Song dynasty. Around 1230, Koreans invented a metal type movable printing using bronze. This led to the distribution of "Selected Teachings of Buddhist Sages and Seon Masters" in 1377, a Korean book.

The Christian Monasteries carried on the Latin writing tradition in the Western Roman Empire. Before the adoption of the printing press, books were copied by hand, expensive and rare. Smaller monasteries had only a few dozen books, at the end of the Middle Ages, the papal library in Avignon and Paris library of the Sorbonne held only around 2,000 books.

The scriptorium of the monastery was usually over the chapter house where artificial lights were forbidden for the fear of fire done only in day-light by enthusiastic students...

What I fear more are the lunatics in power. I know of many examples, In 367 AC, Athanasius, the zealous bishop of Alexandria issued an Easter letter in which he demanded that Egyptian monks destroy all such unacceptable writings, except for those he specifically listed as 'acceptable' even 'canonical' — a list that constitutes the present 'New Testament'. When the burning of books is widespread and systematic, like the burning of the Library of Alexandria in 49 AC, or the destruction of Aztec codices by Itzcoatl in 1430s, and the burning of Maya's indigenous American civilizations manuscripts on the order of bishop Diego de Landa in 1562.

We still find the lists of forbidden books by Inquisition within the archives of Vatican - in 1585 Complete works of Dante Alighieri, in 1600 the complete works of Bruno Giordano and Nicolaus Copernicus, etc.

"I have a good news, the great supporter of Christianity Paul Siu again resumed the high offices and is now in charge of the Chinese Calendar reform." I shared the letter that I have received just that morning.

"This will give us a perfect opportunity to demonstrate our good will to Chinese governors, to offer the secrets of Arabic and European science in return for protection and the right to preach Christianity in China." Said Ottavio.

"There is more to it," I said, "Johann Adam Schall von Bell, a great friend of mine, the head of our mission was asked to replace his predecessor Schreck who was gravely ill in the work of reforming the Chinese calendar. This task is far removed from his ordinary duties of the apostolate but he is an honest man and he understands that in its success lay the future of the mission."

Father John Adam was a highly educated man born in a noble family in Cologne. His voice, looks and movements mirrored his background, love for studies and Jesus. He was a young Jesuit when he first arrived to Macao in 1619, when we were still deeply troubled by the war waged against us four years earlier by the high mandarin Kio Shin. Four of our chief missionaries could not any longer do their mission and were expelled to Macao. His first 10 years within the mission were troublesome and bear no fruit. Now, in 1630, he had behind him many years of experience of successes and failure of conversion of Chinese into Christianity, he spoke Chinese perfectly, and clearly understood that for us to succeed our approach must radically change.

When he was asked to replace his predecessor Schreck he immediately understood that in its success lay the future of the Christian mission.

"As you know, I spoke to John Adam, that we base astrology on calculation of the movements of planets along the ecliptic."

In Chinese astrology, the lunar zodiac has prime importance, the sky is divided into 28 segments of moons journey through the sky.

The establishment of the Chinese Annual Calendar is one of the most important affairs of the Chinese State. The Board of Mathematicians composing of 200 highly educated members gathers every year to announce the astronomical situation for the coming year. Their task is to build a calendar for the year to come, taking into consideration the days of new and full moon, the times of the solstices and equinoxes, the positions and conjunctions of planets, movements of the sun with the dates of its entrance into each of the twenty-eight constellations that form the Chinese zodiac.

"This Calendar is for the natives extremely valuable." Ama emphasised my point.

"Just yesterday, at Li Po's house, I met one of his friends, a fortune teller and astrologer, he was constructing a personal horoscope for a rich merchant's son. He showed me a rectangular frame-shape grid, he was working on, divided into twelve smaller rectangles. He used both horoscope and the yearly calendar to establish auspicious and inauspicious days in the year, and in the life-time of the merchant's son, to calculate days that are good for his education, marriage, start of business and other family affairs. Looking at the personal Chart and the yearly Calendar, he then calculated days for action and days for rest, days when different Gods are worshiped, and when trouble or luck is more likely to strike. The Calendar is the guide for every single day within the year!" I shared.

"Very important!" Ottavio nodded.

The Chinese astrologers, educated and non-educated people believe that they can calculate the circle of life and death, map each person or event into the horoscope. They all believe in how essential the accuracy of the Calendar is.

Huai Nan Tzu, the ancient Chinese astrological script, groups the stars in five enormous stars constellations. The Heavens are divided into Guardians of the four directional palaces, called: The Green Dragon of Spring, the Vermilion Bird of Summer, the White Tiger of Autumn, the Black Tortoise of Winter. The only one that I could recognise studying the map was the Great Bear that was within the fifth 'palace', called the Central Palace.

Finding a chapter of Huai Nan Tzu that gave Emperors pointers of how to rule the Kingdom and how Heavens behave, I read them out to my friends:

'Men's lives are reflected in the movement of Heaven;
When there is cruelty and violence, there will be violent winds.
When there are oppressive laws, there will be plagues of insects.
The Four Seasons are the Annals of Heaven;
The Sun and Moon are the Messengers of Heaven;
The Stars and Planets record Heaven's seasons;
Rainbows and comets are Heaven's warnings.'

The book also has a guideline for every single day:

'In the time of Chia Tzu, action should be restrained,
In the time of Ping Tzu the worthy should be promoted
In the time of Wu Tzu the old and widows should be cared for, favours bestowed and goods sold
In the time of Keng Tzu walls and barriers should be improved and fortifications strengthened.'
In the time of Jen Tzu close the gates of villages, search strangers thoroughly, execute offenders and close bridges.

We watch the sky all the time, my Chinese friend nodded, noting any changes in the appearance of each and one of the stars. Changes may be in the colour, the position or the brightness and they are all interpreted to mean something specific, an appointed minister will be well liked and respected, a war will break out, a prominent person may be punished for the wrongdoings, the army leaders will die, the earth will be very fertile or destroyed by droughts, crops will ripen to maturity or the harvest may fail.

"To hope to understand the Chinese astrology," I shared my knowledge with John Adam, "we need to understand Chinese symbols, and elements and their interaction."

The accuracy of the Calendar is especially important because the eclipses of the Sun concern the ruler of the country; and those of the Moon concern his generals and advisers and none of them are a good omen that is why a good astrologer needs to precisely calculate both of them.

A typical Chinese calendar-almanac records the days by month, listing auspicious days for journeys, marrying, building houses, carrying on a trade, burying the dead, collecting money, cutting down trees, taking medicine, repairing walls, digging ditches, even sweeping and bathing! Every single activity is enlisted within these calendars.

The Chinese astrology is based on twenty-eight lunar mansions, or Hsiu, the constellations that Moon encounters on its passage through the sky.

Unfortunately, for the Chinese astrologers, finding out the particular Hsiu in which the Moon resides requires long and complex mathematics.

"Since the Chinese year is lunar, New Moon falls always on the first day of the month, and it is shorter than the Western one by about ten days causing the year to 'drift'." Ottavio mused.

"If we make sure that they know that our calculation is superior, Chinese will come and ask for our help." I nodded.

The Chinese astronomers are at the moment incapable of discovering the defects of their methods and calculations, and this was our opportunity to render a service and strengthen our position in China.

"This mission was well understood by our founder, Father Ricci," John Adam told me, "who inspired some of the Chinese philosophers and scientists to start thinking about the translation of the Catholic liturgical calendar into Chinese."

What we need to do is convince the authorities of the errors of their calendar, make them understand that they need us and our calculations.

"To achieve this," John Adam told me, "we will have to design a complete course in astronomy, arithmetic, geometry, and other areas of mathematics. This will be your task, dear Benedict, I will leave it in your capable hands to manage."

So I did. I designed courses, worked on translations, examined the different systems, worked on the merge of the two systems of knowledge.

The wheel of fortune was put into a motion because of a mistake of an hour by the Board of Mathematics in the announcement of an eclipse. We have made sure to warn them that this will happen, and Chinese were surprised to learn that our warning was actually accurate. They decided to request our help.

Many seeds were planted in many minds and the idea of the knowledge sharing became our reality. We all had our own goals, the Church wanted to spread Christianity in China, Chinese wanted to learn a better method for celestial calculations, and the goal of our little group was the interchange of the two scientific thoughts: we had much to learn from each other.

The idea started materialising.

Chinese were open to listening. They were open to learning.

Christians that we approached agreed that this is the way to Chinese hospitality. They were cautious and suspicious at first, of the tools we proposed to use, because some thought, helping Chinese worship their ancestors better, was not something Church authorities are keen on doing; but building their Calendar was building their trust and at that point trust was what was needed to continue our work.

Soon after, John Adam became a trusted counsellor of the new Emperor Shunzhi, he was made a mandarin and became Director of the Imperial Observatory and the Tribunal of Mathematics. His position enabled him to procure from the emperor permissions for the Jesuits to build churches and to preach Christianity.

Within the next fourteen years, John Adam became a very successful missionary.

We managed to convince the Empire to entrust the missionaries with the correction of the Calendar and we started to translate books containing the rules of European astronomy. We worked for years translating precious manuscripts and books into Chinese.

However, not all had the same mission.

Rumours had it that the ships of the English East India Company sailed up the Pearl River and after they were refused trading privileges they went into pillaging and burning of many vessels and villages, spreading destruction wherever they appeared. The Chinese even claimed there were incidences where armed parties of Portuguese soldiers entered into villages and carried off their women, and in revenge they started destroying Portuguese ships killing hundreds of their crew.

"It is difficult to see Christians as anything but savages who cannot tolerate other cultures, Gods, and ways of thinking." Ottavio started one of his arguments about the ways Christians behaved as guests of foreign lands.

"Europeans are acting overwhelmingly rude. The companies act with violence and brutal strength, with no moral values, and are inspired and moved only by money." Ottavio was getting angry talking.

"It is our task to show Chinese the other, spiritual and scientific side of our culture, the side that cherishes philosophy and self-knowledge," I told him.

The prevailing thought amongst educated Chinese is that missionaries are hard to communicate with and very dogmatic. They push the belief that there is no other truth but Christian truth, and this will always keep them apart from the learned classes of China who know better than just to follow a dogmatic view.

In the midst of this turmoil, we were trying to build a new foundation that was supposed to mark the beginning of a new century of knowledge exchange between enlightened minds of China and Europe.

Our method and our prediction soon proved to be true, working on the Calendar was the way to Chinese trust.

By 1634, we helped in translation and printing of around a hundred books containing the arts of European sciences: astronomy, arithmetic, geometry, mathematics and astrology. Thirsty for knowledge that is coming from afar, the Chinese for a moment forgot the hardship that Europeans brought and started to open their, for centuries locked, doors accepting our thoughts and beliefs.

All the provinces of China were soon informed of the important task that was given to the missionaries. The news was received with interest and we were now looked at with curiosity and accepted in many Chinese homes where previously we had no access.

Now, when we are working with the intellectual cream of China on a common goal, on the reform of the Calendar, our reputation strengthened, and the Chinese felt honoured to be in our presence.

"Wherever we go we are greeted with respect, listened to and publicly congratulated. Gospel preaching is allowed in all provinces and the first public church opened in the capital. In just a few years of our work, the Emperor, who I met personally, issued an imperial declaration praising our work. We've even managed to convert ten eunuchs, within the Imperial Palace, laughed Father Schall. This class was the first one to oppose any of our preaching."

This happy progress was for a time stopped by the invasion of the Tatars and the revolution that overthrown the Ming dynasty, and brought Manchu dynasty into power.

At Peking, Father Schall assisted the last of the Ming in his resistance, yet to no avail, the time has come for him to leave his kingdom.

Luckily the Tatars regarded us favourably. Shun-chi, a new ruler was only eight years old when he was proclaimed emperor in 1643.

The minister who governed in Emperor's name for six years confirmed all Schall's powers regarding the Calendar. The young emperor was very curious to meet the missionaries; he loved listening to the tales of the foreign lands that these educated men brought with them and he often called Father Schall to the interviews in his palace. The young Emperor even unexpectedly knocked at Father Schall's door to discuss with him the nature of life, Universe and purpose of all things on Earth.

Shortly after this happy event the new mathematical rules brought in by Christian missionaries to make the Calendar, became compulsory for all the official Chinese astronomers.

The peak of these events was Father Schall's appointment as the president of the Board of Mathematicians.

Our victory was finally real!

The negative seeds planted during the last century, were now uprooted and the seedlings turned to be: understanding and respect.

Seeing what was behind us we now had Hope.

The young emperor, Shun-chi, not only appointed Father Schall as President of the Board, but also gave him high rank as a mandarin to correspond with this important status.

Father Schall was aware that accepting this high rank is a violation of the canon law which forbade priests to hold civil offices and was hesitant of accepting. He tried, for more than twenty years to decline this honour and he told me that he had refused it eight times, that he even pleaded on his knees before the Tribunal of Rites to be released from it, but that he was forced into it to keep the good will of the Governors.

In 1653, as thanks for all the work done in the reform of the Calendar, Shun-chi bestowed on Father Schall the title of *Tung hiuen kiao shi*, "Most Profound Doctor".

John Adam showed me this intricate marble tablet, written in Tatar and Chinese, encircled with dragons and other carved ornaments. For me it was the symbol of all the achievements that we have managed to attain during this time of scientific sharing. Father Schall also got the gift of a new house and a donation for a new church, the first public church that opened in the capital.

But not all were ready for this huge and profound change.

Father Schall's acceptance of the high Chinese official rank, was the reason for much gossip and ethical discussions among the priests in Macao for several years.

A more serious question troubled our missionaries.

How can a Christian Priest be President of the Board of Mathematicians that publishes a yearly Calendar that is full of superstitions and various beliefs that are not in line with the teachings of Christianity?

How can Father Schall stand behind and sign a pagan sacred script that supported worshiping of ancestors, rituals and practices that were not Christian?

How can a Catholic Jesuit Priest head a board that governs practices that are not in line with the Christian scripts?

I'll tell you a story – Ama once told us – there was a very good musician, a flautist, living next to the forest. He was able to play so beautifully that everybody would stop to listen. He was admired by men, by animals and by spirits. He was gifted. He would descend Beauty and Spirit through his music. One day, when he was sitting in the woods playing his flute, wolves, foxes and birds were all peacefully gathered to admire his music, a huge dark tiger jumped out of the forest, surprised everybody, and attacked the flautist eating him alive in a matter of seconds before anybody could utter a word. The gathered crowed was disappointed, astonished and stunned by what has happened. How could you do something like that, didn't you hear how beautiful and heavenly his music was? – they asked in one voice. Music, play, heaven...? What are you talking about, said the half deaf tiger.'

You cannot play music to the deaf, no matter how good you are, the deaf will not hear you.

I was very weary of the deaf.

The audience that reminds me of the deaf tiger is the one that is rough, the one that is convinced that there is no subject that they do not know the best, the one that has closed itself to learning. They are ready to confront you at all times. They are not ready to listen or grow, they are not ready to receive. They like to believe that they own their lives that they can decide, that they can act differently, and yet they are driven by attachments and instincts. Within the infinite number of possibilities for a soul to develop, they always chose the same one – the way of suffering.

Fra Thomas was one of these tigers.

I always knew in advance whether I will meet Fra Thomas that day. An uncomfortable sense of mischievous mystery accompanied his presence and I felt it much before his appearance. My stomach would turn uneasy. Whenever he would plot one of his conspiracies, Fra Thomas was one of my weaknesses.

Finding it difficult to stay calm after any of his visits full of prejudices, fears and failures.

That day he looked as though he is surrounded with a cloud, his voice cold, his brain recalling all the happenings covered with a veil soaked in black.

Once surrounded with that black velvet, the darkness was too concentrated. Living his own Reality that he called the reality of the Church, clenched to despair, where each wrinkle narrated a story of 'I' that does not want to be Awake or Conscious, he hated Ama and the hatred was his Life.

"She is a witch, I am certain of it, and I will do all I can to stop her black magic. And her father is a witch too! All that wealth, what do you think, where is it coming from? It is Devil that helps them out!"

"You remember Ruben, he was like son to me, he is now under her spells and who knows how many other people too. I am here to warn you, I came as a friend, before you become one of them!"

"I know of their wicked work, devouring children and causing sickness and death."

I stopped the time waiting for him to collect.
I stopped the time waiting for Earth to react.
I stopped the time waiting for the critical mass to move the energies into the balance. I looked up into God's eyes and saw nothing, refusing to look at me. The time has not yet come! We planted the seeds for future generations to enjoy. This was not our moment! The time has not yet come!

Humanity was not yet ready to hear.

Fra Thomas, Church and Humanity were too immersed in anger to notice anything else.

Fra Thomas's face, his choice of words, all the 'holy' wars, and the killings in the name of Lord, tortures, prosecutions, Inquisition, they were all gathered there, in front of me, shaping the destiny of the future centuries, within Fear and Confusion.

Taking out from the pocket of his little coat a book, hidden until that moment, his Witch-hunter's manual, he said:

"Do you know what is happening in the main-land? They are all over the place! They fly and meet the Devil every night! It is now the time for us to re-act and uproot this supreme wickedness!"

"You must be familiar with this," he continued reading, as though he was hoping to influence me, change my mind or break the spell I might be under: *'it has recently come to our ears,'* he started reading, *'not without great pain to us, that many persons of both sexes, heedless of their own salvation and forsaking the catholic faith,* **give themselves over to devils male and female***, and by their* **incantations**, **charms**, *and* **conjuring's***,… ruin and cause to perish the offspring of women,…"*

"…that they afflict and torture with dire pain and anguish, both internal and external, these men, women, cattle, flocks, herds, and animals, and hinder men from begetting and women from conceiving, and prevent all consummation of marriage…"

"She is not married, you know that," he said, "and she managed to lure Ruben into her sinful net." I know that, I saw them together!

We looked at each other, measuring words, using them as swords. He carried a shield of intolerance rooted deep within the humanity, its beliefs, its fairy-tales, its myths, its Holy Books, the shield of Separation.

Any reasoning would have been weak against his pain.

My words about fairy tales of witchcraft, about love Ama had for the people around her, about the ones she cured, got scattered and bounced of a wall, returning as wounded birds. The more I said, the more he believed that I am the Witch too, dancing sinful dances on the Full Moon on the Grave Yards, using dead people bones as music instruments.

The era we lived in was not as yet ready to accept our mission, was not as yet ready for such a drastic change, the merge of many into One.

The Humanity was too obsessed with a motion of separation. Our dream of building the critical mass that changes the world's consciousness and its way of behaving, entered the cracks of stones, hid behind the thick evergreen branches, merged with the moon's reflection that observes the river flow, in front of this man with an epithet of dogma steaming revulsion from each of his pores.

We managed to translate and distribute books and open Chinese thought to the Christian thinking, but we didn't manage to open the channels from the other end, our homeland thinking pattern stayed firmly grounded, inflexible and stubbornly rigid.

Even though, within our lifetime, we managed to re-earn the Chinese respect, even though we managed to establish peace, even though we built churches this was not enough.

Fra Thomas aimed a carefully prepared poisonous arrow into my heart saying that the Authorities of the Church in all our work saw failure. The Church was now officially disapproving of our Mission.

"The Chinese continue to follow their primitive rituals and customs and they combine their ancient worship with the Christianity, and this is unacceptable, it is a disgrace and heresy."

"Beliefs in guides and spirits are primitive," he repeated, "predictions are pagan and the Church cannot live in peace with paganism!"

"We have to fight against the old customs within this land for our Mission to flourish! It is not a Christian victory if we co-exist with the old"

Fra Thomas was just passing a message we all feared, the message of the Church that did not want to move, grow or accept.

At the time, with my mind deep within the Mission, it hurt me deeply to see that even here, thousands of miles away from Rome, was difficult to escape the grasp of the Old.

The minds of men were not yet ready to hear.

"To the non-Christians," Fra Thomas was shouting, "we have nothing to say, other than they were given a chance to repent and come to God, but they chose not to."

That month, in 1655, five theologians of the Roman College examined Fra Thomas's accusations and Father Schall was asked to resign from the position of the President of the Board of Mathematicians.

That month, Fra Thomas arrested Ama for witchcraft.

The fortune wheel turned against us.

Its deadly cracks were above our heads and we feared it would crash directly on us.

Years of work and effort seemed to be in vain.

The Galaxies of Human Minds were shaking, we had the support of hundreds of Souls that were born to help the shift, the Lady Science passed to us so many insights, and yet, the Old Structure was not ready to fall.

The history now reads like this: Conflicts between the Chinese Government and th Catholicism that culminated in the 1616, and that were under the control for more than 30 years, were now back at its highest force. High ranking officials advised the Emperor that Catholicism is not respecting Chinese customs and that it should be banned.

By disrespecting Chinese culture we sent out a message of war.

Our protector, Emperor Shun-chi died in 1662 and Chinese arrested Father Schall and myself in 1664. Although they found no evidence of conspiracy, we were imprisoned on the count of high treason and of propagation of an evil religion. Across the country, about 30 missionaries were arrested and sent to the capital for questioning, only a few were allowed to stay outside the city, the rest were deported and imprisoned. Churches were closed down and scriptures burnt.

In 1720, some 50 years after our death, the time carried the same tension between the two, Emperor Yong Zheng passed a law deporting all missionaries from China. Most of the missionaries were forced to flee for Macao, a lot of churches were converted to town halls and schools or torn down. Followers were banned from becoming Catholics again.

Our age, called for martyrs that would die in the process of the reform, sacrificing themselves for the benefit of the future generations.

The success of the Calendar conversion was apparently short lived, yet its effects touched the depths of both civilisations.

Within the mission, during our struggle, I reached the heights climbing the untouchable, and hit the bottom within the darkness of the jail.

After the short trial where everyone including us knew we were guilty, we were condemned to be cut in pieces and to be beheaded.

When I completely gave up, when I surrendered to Death, the Heavens opened to deliver a miracle.

A violent earthquake came over Peking, a thick darkness covered the city, meteors appeared in the sky, with the dark rain damaging a part of the Imperial palace.

Listening to the air filled with the sound of roaring lions and cracking thunders, the end of the world seemed near. The rivers, roads moved and trees got uprooted. Earth's anger was visible everywhere. Chinese feared the worst. They had a fresh remembrance of an earthquake that occurred around a century ago, the earthquake that was still vividly alive within the stories of their grandparents.

That time when Earth bestowed its rightful place amongst us scared mortals, the power of Her dance was such, that the hills that took thousands years to form became valleys in a minute, and valleys that hosted river beds for centuries, became hills. That earthquake was huge, the awakened Dragon hit an amazing area of 500 miles.

The rocks ruptured under the massive burst of energy. No corner on Earth was spared. The elements took their revenge in turns. Water gushed out from underground and fire closely followed it. The winds stormed filling the air with horror. 98 counties and eight provinces were that week visited by Death.

Bodies mixed with debris buried under poorly constructed houses or simply swallowed into the Earth's womb were everywhere. The Chinese that survived could not extinguish the fires for days, and what the fire spared, the floods destroyed, ruining the water supplies opening the door for diseases to quickly spread. A total of 830,000 people lost their lives.

A possibility of history repeating itself was terrifying for the grand-children of the Great Earthquake.

They quickly connected the meteor rain with our imprisonment and in fear of worse calamities, they decided to release both myself and Father Schall. Our death sentence was revoked and we were sent back home.

In the meantime, we sent a statement to Rome explaining what has happened with our mission, and a new commission concluded in 1664, eight years too late, that there was no valid reason for Father Schall's dismissal.

Unfortunately, none of us could turn back the time.

Throughout my stay in jail I meditated about God, purpose of Life and Universe and my karmic pattern within this amazing Mission.

Both John Adam and I, spent our last years separated from the other missionaries and removed from the obedience to the Pope. I lived in Ottavio's household into my old age. I stayed Ama's and Ottavio's faithful friend until the very end.

I left this life some years after Death knocked also onto Ottavio's doors and I left with a determination to return when the time is ripe to reopen my mission.

I maintain that Truth is a pathless land, and you cannot approach it by any path whatsoever, by any religion, by any sect... If an organization be created for this purpose, it becomes a crutch, a weakness, a bondage, and must cripple the individual, and prevent him from growing, from establishing his uniqueness, which lies in his discovery for himself of that absolute, unconditioned Truth... You can form other organizations and expect someone else. With that I am not concerned, nor with creating new cages, new decorations for those cages. My only concern is to set men absolutely, unconditionally free.

Krishnamurti

A Man Trained to Hate

For years I (Fra Thomas, if you wonder about my name) didn't want to meet her, because I believed she had a power of a nymph that attracts her victims and locks them with her beauty taking away the freedom of their free will.

The rumours of the magic, spells and witchcraft that surrounded her, kept us mentally connected and physically firmly apart. Not knowing her gave me strength to attack her and hate her for being what she is. I used every single chance to scold Ruben or any other Christian for seeing her and I used every single opportunity to voice my disagreement when the citizens of Macao followed her.

It was difficult to watch over the moves of Ama and Ottavio de Nobille because their lives were very private.

Ottavio de Nobille was for me a difficult target, because of his wealth and his powerful friends. Some of the very influential and well-known men of Europe and China were on the list of his protectors. Many times I tried to instigate an inquiry against this man, but my efforts were to no avail.

Knowing that Ama was black and that her mother was a slave, I waited for my moment, for Ottavio's death, to take my actions against her.

In the meantime, I followed their friends, prominent missionaries, scientists, government officials, and amongst them Ruben, Benedict and Father Schall closely.

Ruben was like a son to me before the Dutch attack. The amount of converts he had was a beautiful example to other young priests who came to China with the same mission, to spread Christianity and preach Christ's faith. I was always impressed by the strength of his faith and I could not see him losing the sight of Christianity.

When he arrived to Macao he was a very eager young man, completely devoted to Christ, to Jesuits and their teachings. He believed with all of his heart in conversion and together we spent months finding the best ways to deliver non-believers to Christianity. It was Ruben who came to an idea to exploit the fact that Chinese truly believed in the existence of Tao or the true way.

"This belief," Ruben told me, "will open the ears of Chinese to the preaching of the Gospel and to Christianity as a possible true path - the two did not clash, they were complementary."

"Chinese are very systematic in their approach towards morality," Ruben continued devising his theory, "and they firmly believe in hierarchy and order, they believe in the use of reason to determine which way is true, and our entry point into their culture should be this appeal to reason."

"Chinese will see Moses' Ten Commandments as a very systematic way to approaching God," Ruben explained, "so we will have no problem with their introduction."

Using this approach, we were very convincing and Chinese listened carefully to our reasoning; soon we were leaving converts in vast numbers.

Our relationship started changing after the day of the Dutch attack to Macao. I was away on the day of the attack and when I returned I heard amazing stories of his bravery.

It was after the fight that he for the first time mentioned Ama, but it wasn't but after some years that I realized how close to Ama he became. My suspicions were proved by the ever decreasing number of converts he had, and by his final refusal to continue converting Chinese into Christians and his constant wish to instead stay in the monastery and pray.

The only logical explanation for his weird behaviour was that Ama cast a spell upon him.

Years past and no effort of mine was fruitful so during one of our encounters I demanded from Ruben to either leave the Church or stop seeing Ama. To my amazement he decided to leave us both. Hearing his decision, I felt as though I have lost a son.

Ever since, I kept this wound open and the pain burning, looking for a moment I would revenge the loss of this special Soul.

Only once we had a chance to talk face to face, the time I was in her house determined to arrest her, determined to prove her connection with Devil.

A room that looked like a prayer room with an altar in the middle was our battle field. The altar was in a triangular shape, a triangle with all the sides equal. The room was full of astrology symbols.

I knew that Ama was familiar with astrology. I also knew of Ottavio's efforts to reform the Chinese Calendar and I knew that astrology was closely related to this effort.

My excuse for this little visit to De Nobille's household was a research I chaired on alchemy. I used Father Benedict's recommendation so that Ama would invite me into their house.

"As you know," she said, "Alchemy and Magic are female aspects of Christianity. They represent the unknown side, underground methods, daughters, Yin of religious work."

I was going around the room, looking at books that were piled next to the fire place and pictures hanging on the walls, I searched for the forbidden books, for a proof that Ama was a heretic.

"While you, preaching Christianity, work with morals, Alchemy works with the undiscovered side of conscious, the side that is inside the shadow."

The word: shadow, attracted my attention.

She looked at me and smiled.

"Developing female principles," she said, "through understanding myths and magic helps the visible, rational, Yang part of soul development, the religion. A Yin side of the nature always seeks, asks, awakens the Yang counterpart, Christianity and Alchemy seek each other and are closely interlinked."

"Through Christ or through Devil," I asked.

"The goal is the same in both cases!"

I almost jumped out of my skin.

"For Alchemy and Christianity, of course," she continued as though she didn't hear my remark, "the goal is getting closer and closer to God."

"Dismissing magic and damning unknown, proclaiming it Devil's work, we just deepen the gap between good and bad, creating ever stronger differences."

That is why I cannot hate you, you are a part of a God's plan, I could see her eyes telling me. A whore sins because she is labelled as a sinner and she is not given a chance to repent. Because we label her as a sinner, she stays one. All our sinners are sinners because they know not of other ways. Is this for real or am I dreaming? I quickly awoke from my vision and got back to her words.

"Dismissing Alchemy, Astrology, Medicine, Science, Magic, dogmatists turn their back to progress, to evolution, to change."

The dogma ruled behaviours are static, they wither, die, tying knots around their necks, jumping into deep waters followed by a heavy stone of raggedness, inflexibility and lack of wisdom.

Again, I was transferred into a different state, it was my mind talking, not Ama, and yet I could hear Ama's voice within my head.

Look at the world around you, how many boundaries, how many walls, everywhere. Because we define sin so sharply we become sinful and we cannot get out of this circle. Any chemical used in one way can cure a disease but used in another can kill. Christ talked to prostitutes and tax collectors, we don't – we accuse them, attack them, hate them. We see our mischief within them and we cannot live with them within us. Their 'un-holiness' makes us unholy.

Was she casting a spell on me? *In the long run you cannot win, because progress is always one step ahead.* I shook off this vision and came back to the room of our encounter.

She was holding the cross in her hands with the most gentleness.

"The cross will give us freedom. The square that was born out of a circle will give us freedom. Four points will direct us."

"Its secret is not in perfection but in completeness. Everything that is below the abyss carries the imperfection within. The order was established from the infinite and the life of dualities as we know it on Earth begun. Only through us meeting, marrying, merging, we will both reach God."

"A Taoist opens and receptively listens to the Mother Earth, he is tolerant and patient believing that the gateway to the root of heaven is a feminine approach to life, gentle, invisible movement. The adept becomes 'hsien', a person who will never die and he can ride the wind and fly to the heavens forever."

Her words puzzled me. The cross that gives us freedom, duality and God, Mother Earth and the abyss, riding the wind, flying the heavens, of course she was talking about witches!

"Containing the female within the male, black within the white, Yin within Yang, one will reach true unified energy and vitality, one will pass the door of immortality."

"Too many negative thought will kill you," she said, now looking straight into my eyes.

For a moment I felt my shield melting, for a moment I felt my heart opening, for a moment I felt weak. Too many negative thoughts will kill me.. I quickly closed my eyes and re-composed, in fear she is hypnotising me.

I hated her when she talked about Alchemy, I hated her when she talked about Christianity, I hated her when she talked about the Chinese beliefs, even though I wanted to hear just a bit more, hoping that her words will give me more proof of her witchcraft.

"Knowing the strength of a man and keeping a women's care, discovering the fire within the water, becoming a child once more." Ama continued.

Christ did say – become a child! My thought wondered, but I re-focussed again, afraid to lose my hate, breaking her spell one more time.

During that encounter with Ama, I must have uttered many words as a response to hers. Obsessed with my-own mission to destroy this woman. My focus had only one goal, to discover a thief, a liar, a deceiver, a witch, I was looking for a proof that she is a hidden monster that feeds on people's energies and blood, and that we must accuse her and we must stop her.

I must have struggled and enquired and behaved as a child would, full of anger, wanting to prove and fight, being loud and rude and hard, not wanting to understand, not wanting to listen, not wanting to learn.

For some reason Ama offered me a key to the knowledge and this key has haunted me since.

Now, I cannot remember any of my words but that day, I was there to arrest her, and so I have.

Ama did not hate me. On the contrary, I saw love in her eyes. She didn't even see me as a necessary evil. A part of God's plan, a nuisance perhaps, but a part of God's creation. Deep within, I was defeated by the strength of her Purity.

Just in case you still wonder did I manage to do any harm to her or her father or her mission during my lifetime, yes, I did. I convinced the Church officials that the reform of the Chinese calendar was a disgrace and that Father Schall was to be asked to resign and that led to the set of events that have awoken Chinese anger.

Also I managed to imprison Ama for the witchcraft but her imprisonment lasted only a few days during which I didn't manage to conduct any of my enquiries to prove her connection with Devil.

Her influential Chinese friends released her dismissing any court case as illegal since Macao was not supposed to be ruled by Portuguese but Chinese Government. She was out of the prison in no time and I was heavily scolded for daring to detain her.

My death put an end to the futility of my mission whose purpose only God and Ama, at the time, understood.

'He who joyfully marches to music rank and file, has already earned my contempt. He has been given a large brain by mistake, since for him the spinal cord would surely suffice. This disgrace to civilization should be done away with at once. Heroism at command, how violently I hate all this, how despicable and ignoble war is; I would rather be torn to shreds than be a part of so base an action. It is my conviction that killing under the cloak of war is nothing but an act of murder.'

Albert Einstein

A Man Trained to Kill

I got to know Ama during the Dutch attack on Macao, during the 24th of June 1622.

Ama healed my wounds helping me recover after our defeat. I was a soldier of the Dutch East India Company whose fleet attacked Macao that fatal summer day in June 1622. I didn't trust her or anybody else around. I didn't like people and I didn't expect anything from them, I was just waiting for smoke to settle, my wounds to heal, and for time to be alone so I could escape, escape physically cause my mind was locked in chains, and I could do nothing about it.

The Dutch East India Company (for the ones who know Dutch: Vereenigde Oost-Indische Compagnie, VOC) was running the Asian trade routes and they were major political and economic power of the time, establishing colonies, and concluding treaties with Asian rulers.

VOC was empowered to have its-own army, and I was a part of it, to imprison and execute convicts, and wage wars in Asia. As Portugal was 'united' with the Spanish crown, with which the Dutch were at war, the Portuguese Empire was a target for military interventions.

Macao was a thriving port with excellent trade connections, so overtaking it could have meant increasing our domination in the region and further profits for the Company. Just to give you an idea of the Company's monopoly and the power at the time, the statistics say that during the 16th and 17th century, it sent almost a million Europeans to Asia on more than 4,500 ships, working with 2,5 million tons of Asian trade goods.

I had good relations with the 'top heads' of VOC, I was amongst their most respected soldiers, spies. They have entrusted me with a very interesting and an inspiring mission: they asked me to discover the secrets of martial arts that were carefully developed within China for centuries.

As a soldier, I was trained to fight with many different weapons, but observing one of the Chinese fighters I quickly realised that their way of moving the body, their strategy of using opponent strength, their attitude towards the enemy, were more than a fight, they were an art form. Fascinated by this art the mission became my quest and I happily came to China as a spy to steal this fighting discipline from the very best. In Holland, we had arms, ships, canons, but they, Chinese, had a secret to the human body and mind.

My destiny soon led me to the Shaolin monastery in South China that was renowned for its long tradition of Chinese martial arts. In 1610, when I first stepped onto the Chinese ground, China was still ruled by the Ming Dynasty and Shaolin monastery blossomed. In those days, it housed over 1,000 soldier-monks.

As you can imagine, I had a hard time entering the monastery.

The monks would not under any circumstances trust a stranger, a foreigner, a Dutchman. An old local man narrating a fable gave me a key to their doors. According to the legend of Shaolin monks a Buddhist monk called Bodhidharma brought the martial arts from India to Shaolin monastery in early 500s. When he arrived at the temple, he was refused an entry, so he went to a cave nearby and meditated until the monks were convinced of his spiritual eagerness.

Knowing this story, armed with the letter of recommendation from some high Chinese officials, I followed suit using the same technique Bodhi-dharma used to be admitted to the temple.

The recommendation letter protected me from an immediate expulsion but I had to spend weeks that turned into months living in the cave next to the monastery, sitting still, meditating, or training whenever I knew that there are curious eyes observing every movement I made.

Awaking the curiosity of young soldiers monks, intriguing them by the fighting techniques I mastered during my past, slowly I gained their trust with my persistence to stay put until I am accepted to live in the Temple.

After they saw me practicing meditation for hours, sitting still unconditionally, convinced them that even though I am a foreigner, I am keen on learning Zen Buddhism and that my final goal is Enlightenment.

My entrance to the Temple was granted when I coincidently stumbled upon a youth who was hurt, dying with a fever not very far from my cave. I tended his sickness and helped him come back to the Temple. The elders of the Monastery saw this as a good omen, and allowed me to enter the Temple's door.

Before I was initiated into the martial arts practiced within the Temple, more than three years later, I had to patiently await my turn, proving myself to be loyal and trust-worthy. To insure that the art was not abused, it was never documented or given to 'strangers'.

After months spent cleaning and working within the monastery, practicing Chi Gung during the day and meditating at dawn, mid-day, mid-night, I was allowed to participate in the martial arts training.

Chi Gung or what they call the 'energy work' is a mix of minimum effort exercises performed in a focussed precise manner. My previous training relied on speed, power, and discipline, so I found these slow movements, quiet and gentle work-out, fascinating.

Monks were convinced that Chi Gung can heal any disease, and keep the body in a perfect balance. According to them, Chi Gung exercises are essential for developing stability, training body posture and understanding the unity of breath and movements, and for increasing sensitivity.

Not only that, I learned that Chi (Qi) is more than a concept or a method of healing, for the monks, Chi is the vital energy or life force that lives within all of us and it is a physical reality. People, animals, trees, rivers, mountains, planets, stars exist as an intriguingly complex network of overlapping and interacting energy fields. Knowing Chi, was ultimately, knowing God.

When the monks felt that I was fit for initiation, I had to take 36 oaths and 21 moral codes that officially marked me as one of them. Now, I could start my proper combat training. Once I was allowed to practise I learned quickly.

To the monks, my teachers, martial arts were methods to cultivate their mind and nourish their Buddha nature. 'Ming Sum Gim Sing' they would say: understand your mind and see your true nature.

Within the Temple, monks developed a new, high level martial art, gathering all the experience of the previous methods. The elders shared the most advanced knowledge of the human body, of human psychology, and fighting, and they created a completely new style called Wing Chun.

Wing Chun was designed for a single purpose, hand to hand combat. The monks' goal was to in the case of emergency, train ordinary people, even women, to fight very effectively in the shortest possible time. Their goal was to create a martial arts system that was simple and deadly. Every movement of the hands and feet had to be coordinated, precise and powerful and it had to directly apply within a fight.

When I got to know it, I realised why this new art was conducted and passed from monk to monk in such secrecy. It was a supreme art of killing.

Wing Chun is like a divine dance, my teacher said, it is very precise and clear. You do not need all the kicks that you usually find in other Martial Arts, you don't need all the strength, it is design to be effective. Wing Chun does not have fancy stuff around it, no high kicks, and its movements are very refined.

All you need to learn is the 'Five Lines' of human anatomy and you direct your strikes onto the third Yang line. This line is called the "One" line and divides the body into half. This line is the secret line that covers many vulnerable vital points of any human being. Hitting any of them will cause instant disability or death.

It is all about the human sensitivity, my teacher explained, about the flexibility, and coordination of arms and hands. Your opponent would be looking at your hands and your feet would have already broken his knee caps, it is very fast, very effective.

You have to have the knowledge of how to use the force of the opponent against him and how to position your arms, limbs, and body in such a way so that the force becomes explosive. The fights do not last long, they are over in a couple of minutes.

The Hung Fa Yi punch is the most effective because it travels the shortest distance, he said, and is supported by the entire body structure. You will use it, only when your space is threatened, and then all the options are open: kicks, punches, traps, throws. This is one of the most dangerous postures for the combat.

I practiced Hung Fa Yi punch for months and performed it to its perfection. Wing Chun was a perfect combat technique for someone who was trained to kill since the age of 13. My passion for fight was in the past used by the VOC military machine and I was one of their best soldiers, famous for my talents. I knew how to hide, endure hardship, wait, sneak like an animal, and appear un-noticed killing quickly. I had a reputation. The more I was encouraged to kill, celebrated and recognised for my 'bravery', the more I hated myself and humanity that created me.

Even though it is difficult to believe, I was actually once a normal 12 year old boy who wanted to become the best in whatever he was studied, who looked at the shiny armour and dreamt of riding a horse defending his King. I got the armour, I got the horse, but the dream was long forgotten in the river of blood that was floating everywhere I went.

When I left the Temple, I realised that I have become a supreme killing machine.

Every time my space was threatened, my tools would automatically turn-on and my kicks, and punches were mortal.

My mission as a spy was at this point accomplished but I felt that my journey has not yet begun. Going back to Holland was not an option, the work on much more amazing 'machine' started within the Temple, and the work on my 'mind', on my energy force, on my 'Chi' has opened in front of me, showing me an infiniteness of possibilities.

Lost in my thoughts, in my own discoveries of futility of life, its order and its sense, I lied and escaped from myself many, many times. Long time ago I stopped believing in God, in salvation, and in love. Hating others, I hated myself, entangled deep into a circle of defeat. People who saw me as a hero while I was on their side despised me when I rebelled killing somebody I shouldn't have. Their disgust amused me. As a sinner, for them, my best place was in the hands of Death.

Soon after I reported to the Dutch, I was sent with the ship to fight for Macao, where I ended up stranded with the DeNobilles.

After the combat where I was left unconscious on Macao's grounds, Ama healed my wounds. She treated me as though she was my sister, as though she knew me all her life, and as though there is nothing more natural in the world but to spend sleepless nights curing a prisoner, sinner and a slave.

She asked me my name and from then onwards she treated me as a free man and a sin-free soul. Now, this was scary, I just knew that this woman had absolutely nothing against me.

"My bird keeps flying directly towards my cat," Ama said when she met me, "she comes to me only when the cat is in my lap, and lands exactly where the cat sleeps and she keeps exiting her nest only when she hears the cat purring. Just yesterday, I saved her from the cat's jaws, do you think she will ever learn?" She glanced over me as though she doesn't see me and continued: "Or will she stay flying towards the deadly embrace over-and-over-again choosing a completely un-fair fight over her deepest fears, and sacrifice her fragile body within the same attraction a suicidal butterfly enters the flame?"

"Her hypnotic fascination, is so similar to our fixation with suffering that keeps haunting us even though we know we could keep our journey towards the death, long and intense, walking the edge, without falling into the abyss of its shadows."

That midnight, once the sounds died within the house, I left what she called 'my' room, she left it unlocked, and I went into her chambers with an intention to steel some silver so that the money would help me find my way in these foreign lands. To my surprise she was standing dressed beside her door, holding a lantern in her hands, and she looked at me, as though she was expecting me.

Puzzled and encaged, I could have killed her or abused her, but there was no fear in her eyes.

"You will find the best to sell and the finest silver inside this chest of drawers," she said, as though the silver was there just so that I could steal it.

"You can also use this strong cotton bag, to put it all in," she pointed to the large strong hard woven sack.

She behaved as my companion in this crime and in reality I was stealing the silver from her. Like an animal trapped, I saw nobody, I had my martial arts techniques and fear and she had none.

"I will go to sleep now," she said, "so tell me if you need anything else."

"But if you decide to stay, I will teach you how to walk the edge without the need for suffering, it will be my pleasure to have you within our household."

She handed me a lantern, going back to sleep, as though I was her brother coming back from the night with friends, so she is helping me enter.

Minutes passing like seconds and hours like minutes, holding to the lantern she gave me, feeling the candle light entering my Soul, I felt exposed. Every time I tried to put the silver into the bag I felt a knife going through my heart, something braking inside me. *I will teach you how to walk the edge without the need to suffer* I heard her say, over and over again. The whole house was asleep. Peacefully asleep...

I had to understand!

Leaving the sack, the silver, going to 'my' room. I fell asleep repeating '*I will teach you how to walk the edge without the need for suffering*', dreaming that I was crying for hours until the down broke when without remembrance of a dream I entered a firm strong dark slumber that lasted for eternity. Nobody came to wake me up. That day, I fell down with fever and I regained my consciousness and strength 2 weeks later with a clear understanding that I wanted to stay in this household longer.

When I managed to get up and start walking, I became perfectly aware of all my ugliness. Aware of my body that was dirty, tired and abused with the long, heavy journey of lies and killings that I called my life. Aware of the fact that I can hardly look anybody in the eyes and in this household everybody was looking me in the eyes! Their eyes were inquiring about my soul's journey, here on Earth, their eyes were not accusing but inviting into the worlds I had no idea existed.

Within the Monastery, I was learning how to be still and meditate, here I will learn how to start knowing myself.

The process of my transformation was about to start within this chaos called my mind.

I was ready to spend a lifetime to understand!

During the first year of my stay in Ama's household, I was convinced that I am obsessed with the Devil.

Thoughts of all the murders I committed tortured me, made me sick very often, made me cry, escaping into misery to find ways out of the misery, ways of liberation from the states of hatred and resentment towards the world around me and especially towards myself.

The only way that offered any help during those long self-pity days was a hard physical work. I would find myself taking the dirtiest possible jobs, punishing my body and trying to purify myself from sins that now have existed only in my head. The people around me did not condemn me and have accepted me as their equal.

Since I knew no better I developed an obsession with the Devil and I was convinced that the Devil was ruling my heart. I thought that I would never manage to get rid of the grasp of the King of Darkness. When I had enough courage to share this thought with Ama, she just laughed. She narrated a story that happened in India many, many hundreds of years ago.

"I will tell you a story of Krishna, and his main follower Arjuna. Krishna is an Indian God and he was one day meant to keep the guard deep within the dark forest. Arjuna, his main worshiper, got very upset and worried, he didn't want his Lord to get hurt because these woods were famous for the existence of notorious Devils that would attack and kill innocent. Hearing his worry, Krishna smiled and replied, 'Arjuna, I have never created demons and evil spirits.' This puzzled Arjuna, 'then, how can the non-existent demons appear in the forest and attack innocent' he asked his Lord? 'The demon you are talking about is not a demon at all. It is just a reflection of the evil qualities within you, your hatred, your anger, and your jealousy. The anger in you is manifesting as the demon. Its power is increasing in proportion to the intensity of anger within you.' Said Krishna. 'No demon has ever been created by me!"

This was very different from anything I've heard before. Is it possible that Devils exist only in our minds? "And God, what about God?" She smiled and left, I was not as yet ready to hear the answer to that question...

Looking at the paintings of Krishna, a blue skinned young Hindu God playing his flute, a shepherd boy lost in the game of life and laughter, surrounded with many forest beings or Dakinis in love, I tried to connect with his lightness of Being. With his pearl ear-rings, head scarf decorated with diamonds, a happy God, not disturbed by Devils, evil spirits, or negative thoughts, seeing Life as far too interesting to waste ion worries and decay. From that point onwards, I asked all to keep calling me Krishna.

One of the first lessons within the Shaolin Temple, during my life in China, and within this magic house, was an elaborate lesson about the concept of Yang and Yin.

"Krishna, how are your Devils?" Asked Ama teasingly.

"I have troubles with all my little Devils (I was now amused calling them this way), with hatred, self-pity, attachments, desires and I am yet to learn how to transform them into their positives."

Waking up in the middle of the night tortured with one of my previous 'kills', I run, disappeared, surrounded by two, three, four of them, my fighting mechanisms kicked in again and I fought killing them all.

I would have probably given up if I wasn't, every now and then, rewarded with a feeling of complete bliss and peace. This timelessness detached and fulfilled essence after a heavy day's work or a day spent walking in the woods listening to crickets, would take me by surprise like a lover would, gently leaving me fragile but alert.

"Can it be that by the act of physical isolation I open a channel that hides unseen at the bottom of the sea, to our ancestor's accumulated wisdom?" I asked Ama.

"Your initiation has started at the Monastery," Ama replied, "now you will experience the transformation."

"I will tell you another story," Ama narrated one of her stories during one of her story-telling evenings at Ole, "it is a story of a very popular Indian saint called Milarepa. Milarepa lived around 600 years ago, she said.

His father was a wealthy, influential man. When Milarepa was still a child, he grew ill and accepting his imminent death, he called together his family and told them that he is leaving all his possessions in hands of his brother until Milarepa grows older. After the father's death, however, Milarepa's greedy aunt and uncle, divided the estate, forcing Milarepa's family to live with them as slaves. They were forced to work hard, exchanging their work for bits of food and some clothing.

Milarepa's mother was desperate for a revenge, so when Milarepa was old enough, she sent him to learn black magic. Milarepa was a good student and to please his mother he managed to create a disaster for his cousins at the family wedding. All the relatives who have been cruel to him while he was a child gathered at the wedding. The magic casted by Milarepa, forced the horses kept outside the main entrance to ran into the main supporting column of the house and the house collapsed killing everyone inside. Milarepa saw the blood-shed that he created and was not pleased. The ghosts of his dead relatives started haunting him.

Milarepa's mother liked the display of the boy's power and did not understand the menace of his action. Once more, she demanded Milarepa's help asking him to protect her against the neighbours who were mistreating her. He launched a powerful hail storm on the area, ruining all the crops. After the storm he saw that the fields of grain were destroyed, many of the animals were killed and that even birds perished in the storm. This greatly disturbed him and he decided to try and find a teacher who would help him save his Soul.

In search for help he became a student of a famous Yogi called Marpa. Marpa knew there was a great deal of evil karma to be worked out so he asked Milarepa to build stone structures on high rocky hills only to have him tear them down again, and start the work from scratch. Marpa was also very short tempered with Milarepa shouting at him and beating him for every mistake.

After this hardship was over Marpa gave Milarepa instructions in the methods of meditation.

Learning how to meditate, Milarepa vowed that the life of meditation was the only path for him. He spent years meditating in a cave. It is believed that Milarepa is one of the rare saints that managed to reach enlightenment in a lifetime."

So I have a chance, if Milarepa managed to get enlightened, I still have a chance... I muttered.

From that day onwards, I asked all to call me Milarepa.

Through the purification, I tried to understand the nature of sin and why it was so natural for a human being to be negative. Easier said than done!

"Happiness is a choice," Ama looked at me with her sparkling eyes, "a conscious choice!"

"Tell me Milarepa, do you think that you push yourself into Unhappiness?"

"Like your cat or your butterfly," I reminded her of her allegory that was still alive in my memory even though many moons have gone by.

"It is a misconception that happiness is a gift, it is a choice!"

But what a difficult choice! I almost screamed...

Many years of evolution taught us, people, how to preserve energy, how to walk easier roads and how to survive with as little effort as possible.

It is in our code to go into inertia and laziness if the circumstances let us.

It is the same with any animal, many will let you overfeed them and in the process become very fat, lazy and slow.

Our animal, survival instincts will tell us, indulge, use the opportunity. We become a machine that wants to indefinitely.

The inertia leads us into depression and to learn how to avoid the pattern of becoming a slave of instincts, laziness or sleep, we have to work hard in training to love.

To choose Happiness as the way of Living, I need to train Love. I repeated slowly.

In the same way you were once trained to kill, now you need to train love. Ama affirmed.

To choose Happiness as the way of Living, I need to train Love.

I've heard of yogis that managed to keep their bodies without any sleep or food for days, and the legends say that they still could feel strong and healthy just gazing at the sunlight and meditating. My experience thought me that not all of us can be yogis! My exuberant fasts and hours of not sleeping just led me to different types of sickness. My Soul wanted to find a different way.

My lesson was that the body temple needs nourishing, a proper balanced diet, rest and action. Like with machines that have to be maintained every day I had to learn to be aware of my actions and chained reactions.

Knowing that I don't know, I started listening to what is happening within my head. Listening to thoughts is a difficult and troublesome process

So, I spent years learning 'remembering'.

In the middle of my meal, leaving hunger behind, leaving tension behind, leaving gluttony behind, I would find pleasure in the food.

Stopping in the middle of a conversation or heated argument, observing people that were talking, I would deliberately walk barefoot through the woods, or wear minimum clothing when it was cold, observing my eagerness or hate, asking myself: who is it that is angry, who is the one that is sad, who is the one that hates.

One day I started hearing my thoughts.

The thoughts most difficult to fight were the petite ones.

I struggled.

They would creep in to my head as worms, slowly and almost unnoticed but they would multiply fast and take all the space, becoming the centre of me and my life, causing sadness and anger.

In the same way I was once trained to kill, now I trained to love.

The thought that I am a sinner and that everybody around me is a sinner separated me from Love towards people around me. The hate towards sin was the gatekeeper I couldn't pass on my way to Love.

"Through the development of virtues your Mind gradually 'whitened'," Ama explained years later, "through the constant struggle with instincts, where 'I' breaks into many pieces, your 'I's changed. I saw you changing through all these years.
"

Try with this thought, Ama said, try with: I am not any better or any worse than anybody else around me.

Neither better nor worse! Experimenting with this thought was challenging especially when a beggar or a leper or a madman would knock on our door. Nobody is any better or worse than I am. Nobody! I looked at their dirt, sickness, separation from life, at rotting wounds pushing my disgust to extremes and thought, I am not any better or worse than you. Somewhere behind that battered and abused life-form that does not look human any more is a Soul that is no different than mine.

Prompted by Ama, I meditated on Christ or Buddha or watched great men speak. Wow! A little me is not any worse than kings and priests or any other human being! That was a tough one.

"Teach me about Awareness." I asked my Dakini.

"Walking through Life asleep, demands less effort. It is easier to say 'Only God knows why this has happened! Once you are in the state of awareness, you are exactly where you are supposed to be. Indeed, God does know why something has happened! You as a Soul, descended through Spirit, knows exactly why certain things are good for you.

The Remembrance brought back the pain.

"One thing to remember is that God will always give you more than you can take. The circumstances around you constantly change so that you can learn how to respond to them, if your Soul doesn't find challenges and does not feel that it is growing, improving and progressing, it will create the challenges that might destroy you." Said Ama.

Following own path of purification, after many, many years, I have again fallen violently sick secretly hoping that Death will bring me closer to the union with God, with Love and Spirit and Light.

Ama was next to me, looking at me, with the same eyes of recognition and the spark of inner joy that recognised my secret plans.

"Purity is not enough," she said nursing me, "you have to continue moving because the force is invoked and if this power is not used for Light, it will change into its opposite, it will be used for demolition, consumption, extinction, death." "In the process of transformation after black becomes white, white has to become yellow and then red, the energy of fire, it has to become Sun itself. It is your time to become Sun." She trusted my strength.

Another time she said: "After whitening when the male and female principle within you merge, you will became a vehicle of pure force, crimson is born and that crimson produces gold."

The new self is full of energy that is fire, firm like earth, flexible like water, and light as air. Alert and playful one becomes the philosopher's stone, changing myself, I acquire the power to change others.
"At the very beginning, when I first met you, your 'I', your body, and emotions, and your mind, they all worked against your spirit, closing the passageways to the Soul's expression, leaving it isolated, alone and hidden. You have been imprisoned and you suffered and your Soul was a captive of your desires, bound to the wheel of life. Winning back your divine nature, building your own core of awareness and light was a fight worth fighting.

There is a spiral movement in our spiritual development and this spiral can at times feel discouraging. Yet, Light unfolds, bringing your Soul out of imprisonmen, your Soul catches that Light and that is how you yet again gain freedom."

The Soul, now full of light, screams: awaken!

"Your Soul wants to go through the last stage of the alchemical re-birth: through the resurrection. Here, in China, it is believed that the alchemist overcomes the limits and ascends to higher states becoming a *Zhenren* or Authentic Man. You can become a zhenren gaining the power to stop the cycle of Life and Death.

Your death is in your hands!"

Compassion for all the living beings in the Universe.

All through my life I felt that sickness was my escape. My body would become weak and painful swimming in this deep swamp of muddy waters of unconsciousness. Life was not easy to live. This time, I felt it hard to imagine that I will wake up tomorrow. Hard to look at the world that is full of suffering and love this Divine play of energies as a part of the same coin.

However, I owed this last try to Ama, I owed her the trust that she had in me, so I broke through the clouds of self-inflicted torture that felt very comfortable and safe.

I was re-born to help her in her mission.

It was a beautiful spring day of 1630, and I've been in Ama's household for over 7 years. Ruben left Ama's life a year earlier and I felt Life and beauty flowing through my veins.

That day's spring breeze found a mission in destructing my focus, one moment, I stared at the moon, another, observed the cherry blossom, or smelled my favourite rose - Moon.

Ama was with me chanting about her favourite, the secrets of the alchemy of the soul: "Your body is a chariot, horses are thoughts and emotions, and the charioteer is the soul. The chariot, horses and the charioteer, a body, mind, and soul, they all play a role in the speed of our movement towards enlightenment and the state of happiness we are able to achieve. If the horses lead the journey, the chariot might never move or it might move too fast or take the opposite direction; and if the horses are strained or abused they might die of exhaustion before reaching the destination;"

"If they are let loose they will stop to eat, sleep, they will fight and will not care less about the charioteer." I added playfully, following her little comparison.

"Correct, if the mind is let to rule, it will behave as wild horses, it will disobey, struggle and possibly kill the charioteer."

"If the chariot (our body) is not in a good condition, it will break during the journey, and no matter how good the horses are, the speed of the chariot will diminish and the journey might end before its time." I added listening to her giggle.

"Correct, body has to be respected..." She added flirtingly.

"Can I now respect your body", I leaned to touch her belly. Dancing with words.

"Across the stones and through the deep waters, inevitably breaking my wheels, always cursing God for it." My hand has disappeared inside her blouse.

"Better ever than never," said Ama. Putting her hand onto my lips, her touch was enchanting. This was the closest we have ever been to each other.

"The soul, how do I listen to my soul? I asked moving a step forward, allowing her to feel my heart-beat.

For a moment, that lasted an eternity, we were close enough that I could hear her heart-beat.

"During my strenuous training, I got used to ice baths to strengthen my body's response to colds and diseases. More physical work made me stronger, I moved my threshold of hunger, but now I wish to explore SeX, I whispered in her ear."

"Every single day we are given a choice to make or break the mechanism that is given to us to survive!"

"The body's limits should always be challenged and pushed a step further but steps should be small and done one by one, because jumping two at the time can cause a fall..." She retreated in a playful game.

To understand my chariot was a life-long task, the task that needs a strong Will Power, so I thought: finally, this one is within my powers, not a problem at all.

A merge with Cosmic Love and Cosmic Light, my essence wished to merge with hers.

She looked at me, believing in the powers I never knew I had.

"I met many followers and a few leaders and leaders are always worth fighting for," Ama said.

My Warrior of Light, please, from now on, call me Vishnu. It is Light that will transform me, Pure Light.

This Web felt as a living creature difficult to understand and visibly catch.

Knowledge at that time enters freely.

The True Self is centred in Love.

If you realise your True Self, **you will not need suffering**, you will understand what a waste of time suffering is, when Consciousness can be your choice. On the opposite scale of suffering you will find Love. So, to stop longing for the states of suffering, we need to actually train ourselves in loving! We need to learn to breath Love, speak Love and be Love every single moment of our lives. Love controlled by Will.

"Train me Love, my princess, whisper about Love." I demanded. "Talk to me about Being in Love, about the Merge of the Black Queen and White King," Blowing words into her ear.

"Love is supreme, it expands and overcomes boundaries, it melts all it touches." her hips were around mine.

"When I met you, my life changed." My breath caresses her neck.

My arms were now firmly nested inside her dress, I pushed her body close to mine, our blood pulse, our breath became one.

"Love is not something foreign or external," I took Ama taking her shiver into my Being. "God gave us love, but it is not true that He or She has ever taken it away from us. Not true." I moaned. "Remember it…"

Learning how to love I offered a prayer so deeply devout to Her Majesty, to Venus, to the Goddess of the Sea. I offered the prayer like a simple man, waiting for a swift punishment, repentance and I got none, just the deliverance and joy of a newly found child.
My wilful disobedience carried me into the continents where God does not reign, where the crown is on Her Majesty head.

"Do you feel the Love's flame burning our bones," I asked Ama, not letting her move away from the magic of my touch. "Wonderfully warm with full chests, your strong spine, silky skin, your excitement to meet me carried within the scent of roses."

Deep within I know that Love is the answer to my urge to merge with One.
May the grace of Love of the stars be yours. I kissed her left cheek
May the grace of Love of the winds be yours. I kissed her right cheek
May the grace of Love of the waters be yours. I kissed her forehead
In the name of the World of All Life, Let you become Love. My lips met hers and disappeared within so much expected kiss that took us into a journey around our little planet Earth.

Uplift the heart and feel kisses of stars and breathe of angels upon your body, She is around.

Force and fire, beauty and strength, laughter of delight and souls filled with divine drunkenness, her nature is Love, her blood is immortal divine nectar, Ambrosia that brings eternal life, through Her Beauty the wonder of the Universe opens in front of my eyes, she gives unimaginable joy and to love her is better than all things.

Her body is a palace of which each stone is a separate jewel and I marvel it and worship it, one by one. Her presence is the very light of God and my thoughts are smitten dead before her.

To lie in her bosom, feel her hands, smell her scents, to come to her joy, to love her, to yearn for her, to merge with her, I live. Becoming pure for her, I give, open and dissolve, I befall innocent, transparent, newly born.
Invoking Gods I drink her, love her, disappear in her, for beautiful she is, desirable and in union with her, I enter Understanding.

Rejoicing within the secret temple of her body, eyes burn with desire, for she is Life and Love, our bodies are one, our minds are one, our love is one, Separation becomes Unity.

Yin merges with Yang in the sacred union of a man and a woman. The tiger meets the dragon, water mixes with fire and the woman becomes one with the man dancing in the act of making love. We complete each other and our exchange creates a perfect harmony.

Awakening the original Self I immerse myself within her, she is my guru, I am hers and we are devoted to the eternal joy of bliss.

Becoming one with the great rhythms of nature, free from desires, we both become perfect. The union of Shiva and Shakti release the nectar of purest gold within our bodies and this gold, as radiant as sun is the elixir of immortality. The end of our union is in pure bliss, pure joy.

The Light glows ever brighter, all my senses unsteady, smitten with ecstasy, I am the Lord of Light, Love, and Life, flowering the influence of Sun, staying eternally young, innocent and beautiful, dancing the dance of the creation of the Universe.

Rays from our bodies pierce in every direction inviting the Lady of the Stars to join our dance, we are not each one, nor two merged into one, we are all that was and will be ever created on Earth.

We are, what we are supposed to be all the time, what we are born to be, bright Gods, feeding on delight!

I am not my body any more, I detach observing two bodies completely immersed in their love play. With her hands she held his face, her hair caresses his hands, their lips merged together gently and strong, inseparably, completely tinted with an elixir of love. Their faces mirrored bliss and with every movement they danced extreme love they felt for each other.

Merged in One in the dance of creation, disappearing for the world around them, knowing only the other and this divine ecstasy, her belly button was touching his and her breast were pressed against his chests, her nose against his nose and forehead against each other, in an embrace that lasted eons.

A passer-by, many centuries later saw their materialised image through the Galactic space and time, and in an amazement whisper 'Look at that rock, doesn't it remind you of two lovers merged together.'

Worm and soft were their hands, softer than touch of any silk speaking of adoration, complete giving, absorbed in the love play. She was his and he was hers and they were not in their bodies any more, many became One and One divided into many and they knew, finally they knew, what it is like to be one with God. Flowing, overflowing, disappearing, breaking all known-s to enter into Life pure, innocent, and without fears, dissolving the limits of time. Two, fused in one, got the power of many, liberated within their own creation.

Expanded beyond this Universe, in Silence and in Screams, they thought each other the mystery of Being.

His erection was strong and he was moving slowly, relaxed and in controlled manner, vitality and energy encircled them and they were spontaneity, naturalness and freedom.

Their hearts beat faster, the faces blush and energy flows in waves, revealing mystical moments of two souls merging together. She became his Highest Priestess and he became her Master and Supreme Lover, they initiated each other in the mysteries of Love.

Finding each other they found what is dearest to their hearts, that opens them and inspires them to experience vastness and strength of the most powerful energies of the Universe.

The heat building and rising up the spine to the brain, giving both a sense of bliss. Playing gently, unhurried, resonating perfectly they lived within the beauty of their merge. After hours of this perfect Unity where Will is no more and breath becomes like the one of a baby within a womb, they became Immortal.

She as a cosmic creative force of birth and re-newel, receiving his energy, his fire, his strength, openly and lovingly, closing the circle between the two, Yin and Yang of the Universe.

Subtle as Earth, imperceptible as Water, bright as Fire, free as Air, infinite as Space we became One. Transcending all elements belonging to this world, helping metals become its higher self, become gold, speeding the time, moving through the space, achieving immortality within the merge of two.

It was two years after our first merge when Fra Thomas visited us with his personal mission to arrest Ama accusing her of witchcraft.

In Ama's household among many other books I found the book you all already heard about, the Hammer of Witches, the manual of the witch hunters that in details explained the process of the witch hunt.

*The **method** of beginning an examination by torture is as follows:*

*First, the jailers prepare the implements of **torture**, then they **strip the prisoner** (if it be a woman, she has already been stripped by other women, upright and of good report).*

*And when the implements of torture have been prepared, the judge, both in person and through other good men zealous in the faith, tries to persuade the prisoner to confess the truth freely; but, if he will not confess, he bid attendants make the prisoner fast to the **strapped** or some other implement of torture.*

And, while he is being tortured, he must be questioned on the articles of accusation, and this frequently and persistently, beginning with the lighter charges-for he will more readily confess the lighter than the heavier.

But, if the prisoner will not confess the truth satisfactorily, other sorts of tortures must be placed before him, with the statement that unless he will confess the truth, he must endure these also. But, if not even thus he can be brought into terror and to the truth, then the next day or the next but one is to be set for a continuation of the tortures - not a repetition, for it must not be repeated unless new evidences produced.

Ama warned me of Fra Thomas.

He was never my favourite, he reminded me of a headless chicken running in circles, still believing it's world is the world of living.

That day, he came to arrest Ama and Ama, my love, my soul-mate did not allow me to interfere.

I could have smashed him as a fly, with one hit of the palm against the wall, I could have thrown him out and waited until he returns with many more men that claim that they have the authority to arrest, torture or kill the innocent, I could have waited for them all. I could have given my life for Ama if she just allowed me to do so.

But the evening before Fra Thomas came to our house, Ama told me about the re-building of my Web and the task that I had in this life-time.

"You have to," she said, "re-build the Web that you have so carefully constructed in your previous life, the life of a murderer, the life of somebody who does not like people, who can kill and hurt others without any hesitation."

The key of all my efforts was in changing this Web through changing violence into non-violence.

The violence that was breastfed into my Being since the very beginning of my journey on this little blue Planet was within this Web, the violence that is the main theme of our Religious upbringing. My task was to act differently, to attempt to uproot this violent behaviour from my personal Web.

Understanding the Web and its influence, constantly changing its structure, hoping that one day a new re-born field will face me offering me a chance to act differently. In the same way I was in the past trained to kill, now I was training how to live life without violence.

"What you need to understand," Ama said, "is that you are not re-building only your Web but also the Web of your ancestors, your family, your neighbours, your surroundings, your offspring, the Web of the whole world with its core within the militant and insensitive."

My personal war against my negative conditioning grew into the war against the Humankind's strong predisposition to kill if we believe the cause is just.

She took me aside whispering: "Promise, you will not, under any circumstances, go back to the world of killing. A Warrior takes a responsibility for his acts and the intent of NOT KILLING is so very important. With the fulfilment of this promise you will also change the world of similar behaviour around you. Keeping the promise you help the humankind get rid of the thirst for killing."

Fra Thomas wanted to take her that evening, to put her in a prison, to torture her, with a wish to kill her, and I was there watching this little man, and listening to the strong impulse that was guiding my being: This time it is RIGHT to kill!

All these years Ama trusted me. She trusted my Light and left me to develop within the glow of Her enlightened being. Now she needed my response, to save her meant going back to the Web, to save her meant I would betray her guidelines, break the promise, jump out of the Path, go back to the violence, and all of my being wanted to so -: go back to the violence! My Soul was bouncing in a dance of opposites, in a dance of white and black. God sent me Fra Thomas, the temptation too difficult to face.

Coming out of the room hearing his words of the arrest with only one thought: I am here to save you my love, I will not see any authorities torture you, I don't give a damn about the Web, I will change your destiny, the world does not need such beautiful martyrs. With a simple wrist movement, Fra Thomas will no longer belong to the Land of Living, he will go to Hell, where he belonged to. Soon, I might follow him there too. In fact, if we meet again, up there, me and Fra Thomas, in the midst of the fire, I will still chase him and kill him if he even dreams of hurting you. She was more precious than all the eternity of Hell.

I had no doubts, determined in the righteousness of my act!

Within the next scene that unfolded in front of me, Ama stood a few centimetres away from me. Our motion slowed down as though somebody touched us all with the magic wand. I could feel myself losing the power, feeling my legs becoming heavier.

She raised her hand and the silk of her dress rubbed against my cheek, she touched me in between my eyes and this touch was the last one I could remember. Within seconds everything ceased to be, unfolding the secret of my Life. I saw a point of dense, brilliant light growing brighter and stronger in the centre of the dark that surrounded me.

The light was coming from the centre of the earth, entering my body as a breath of fire. My spine, my bones, the skull, jaw, and teeth, my muscles, they were all shaking, receiving this divine flow. The divine energy was entering my system forcefully, with great power expanding. The energy was coming down from the sun, moon, planets, and it was bright and luminous, powerful and warm. Lost within this expanding consciousness, within love, within this living golden fire I saw a vision, a woman of indescribable beauty.

"A Warrior chooses his path and he follows it unconditionally," Ama said. "Un-conditionally..."

This was the day of my final transformation.

There was no person on Earth that I trusted and loved more dearly than Ama, there was no person whose opinion meant more to me than hers. Ama gave me a chance to understand the difference between human love and Divine Love, a chance to bring this experience to the Web of Humankind.

I am since long dead but my eyes stay fixed on this little blue planet just in case She decides to return, sheltered by Her wisdom, I might be able to surrender to Her path to its very end.

*'However much we have drifted on the ocean of suffering,
today we see clearly that there is a beautiful path.
We turn toward the light of loving kindness
to direct us.'*
Anonymous

Lilith

All through human existence you have faithfully worshiped me and my powers, worshiping your own weaknesses. Stronger your limitations, stronger the manifestation of my powers.

All through human existence you carefully collected the dust of my feet and distributed it among yourselves, whispering stories of my victories, feeding on the grossest parts of my reality.

All through human existence you adored me and evoked my presence addicted to my being, my shrouds of secrets, and shadows.

Only a few manage to turn away from my gaze and look at the light that lives around me. As a gate-keeper of the worlds of darkness. I exist within your minds and am worshiped more than any other God.

Where there is Life, and there is Consciousness, I exist.

My name is Lilith, and I am Adam's first wife and was thrown out of Paradise because I refused to surrender to him. Refusing to live with Adam, I chose a life with demons, with whom I have innumerable children. God sent his angels to find me and with them a punishment, one hundred of my children were killed each day. This made me mad with grief and that is when I decided to retrieve into the shadows of your minds.

Like my sister, Kali, the black Indian Goddess who drinks the blood of her victims and wears human heads around her neck, I also wear a terrible mask of suffering and Death. I am otherwise known as Black Moon, the one that creates and destroys Life, the raw, untamed, murky secret of your own nature, the suppressed, shadow-side of your personality, your deep desire to separate from God and live in my embrace, suffering.

Facing me is not easy, because I awaken within you all your fears, the dark becomes darker and your demons multiply, shaking the very essence of who you are, who you were and who you would like to be.

If you feel doubt, withdraw, if you feel insecure, withdraw! Facing me, understanding me, to finally detach from my powers, is the road of the Warriors and only the Determined will have an access to it. This is the road of the few.

To discover me, you will need to put away the idea of two and be of one body, entering into the road of your hidden nature, the nature that worships Suffering.

The rhythm that led to Her was hypnotic, Ruben felt it within his bones, magical, it was the rhythm of his dreams. As in a dream, hearing drums in the background, feeling secure and loved for the last time, feeling sorrow creeping into my heart, knowing that the time has come to enter a different world, the world so well-known and yet so mysterious, she invited me to step forward and enter the greatest mystery of the human existence, Her world, the world of Lilith.

To take you away from familiar faces, familiar sounds, touches of console, and the remembrance that you are not alone, that is my mission. In my world, Light will disappear. On this journey, you will become one with others vibrating bodies, your brothers and sisters in sorrow, you will merge with them. Prepare to receive the energy of fear and awakening, of burning tension of final initiation.

To learn the secret, you will become one with men living around you, now and 100s of years ago and 1000s of years ago, one with their lives, with their sufferings, with their fears.

I was waiting for you, so many years, with the cup that you called for, so that you could get to know the bottom, get to know me, Black Moon, Black Mother, Lilith.

Let's enter into my stage and peek into one of Many heads.

The name you know, it is Ruben! Step forth so all could see.

The only thing he knew is that he was surrounded with clouds of despair, experiencing the end of his worlds. He was within, what he called 'his body', at the edge of a cliff, above the sea, wanting to die.

And even though he was experiencing misery, desolation, hopelessness, he felt one with the beings around him. Thoughts, worries, life with its past, future and present, everything disappeared. He was a part of one body that danced in a circle finding its cause, moving towards the end of life and creation, going back to the beginning, to its Creator.

Put away the idea of Many and be of one body!

Drink from my essence, from the very source of pain, from the cup that is specially prepared for you, Ruben, carefully taking care of your-own weaknesses.

Ruben listened to the wind hauling through the cliffs and he heard Ama's voice breaking through his storm and there was Aum in Her voice. 'You are now on-your-own!

He looked around his-isolated-mind and he took Lilith in, seeing people around, familiar faces and strangers, looking, as though they know him, each one with a different experience of the same suffering, each one with a wound that still needs healing.

Within my nightmare I got surrounded by abandoned babies, separated lovers, abused children, bruised mothers, liars, murderers, sickness, broken bodies, refugees, burnt houses, miscarriages and loses, Death in Her many forms, surrounded by pain, pain everywhere, from the very beginning of time, to its very end.

My tremble entered the space of no shame and no return, I became one with Many that surround me, one with you that so much hope that you will escape from this bitter cup.

I was a baby almost choked to death by its umbilical cord and the words whispered to me were 'Fight or you will die, breathe or this will be your last breath, you are alone.!'

I saw people being cruel to each other, screams, violence, abuse, selfishness, ignorance, sickness and slow decay, Death laughing at her victims day after day, forever.

I was surrounded by suffering. 'We are sinners that are here to suffer and we need suffering to grow', words resonated within me uttered at the locked entrance of the Garden of Eden.

I looked into Lilith's eyes and her face was so well known, it was so much a part of me.

I did not ask 'why me?' because today, in the shadow of the sea underneath me, I was not alone, I could almost touch the ghosts veiled in pain, deep, heavy, dark pain, that follows us through the very start of our existence.

A woman that came to confess, many moons ago, was in pain because her husband left her. 'I cannot be with you', his blood stopped circulating. She gobbled the last breath of air left in the room, waiting to see what will happen next. Her heart stopped beating allowing a strong stream of pain to pierce her chest, as though somebody has hammered a long, sharp, iron nail straight into her Soul.

I screamed in amazement, the woman changed her appearance into Ama and her husband changed into me, I was the man hammering her Soul...

Everything around her became a motion, slow motion.

She could see in his eyes that there is nothing she could do, that the mortal act was put in place by a force unknown to them all. She felt love, and hurt at the same time, she felt violent, and lost in a wish to kill him and herself. Their dreams pulsated for a moment, disappearing, dissolving fast as though they have never existed, and she caught his hands, looked deep into his eyes and heard him speak about love that will last forever.

The world stopped.

In the middle of her pain, I was left alone.

Why couldn't we be together? Why I had to go through the separation with my flame soul that completes the story of two halves of one joined soul, my polar opposite, with whom I had an instant connection and attraction. Zeus split the lovers in half, condemning them to spend their lives searching for the other half, and I found my half just to leave it to another endless search.

When we were together, and that was virtually all the time, everything seemed in balance. Our souls were learning things in similar ways, we liked the same things, we read each other's minds, we moved in the same direction. All of us, our friends and our families, and people we met coincidentally knew this as our truth from the very moment they met us, we were made to walk this Path together.

Isn't it possible to re-live everything from the beginning, to stop the time, to change the place, to re-construct the end? If we are destined for each other, why can't we just Be Together?

I fell on my knees, begging for forgiveness, understanding and mercy, I will now do anything she wanted, but I felt 'now' was a moment too late. Emptiness and sadness overcame me.

Why is it so important? I could hear Ruben of 10 years ago asking in amazement. Isn't all of this just a game, a procreation game? If we build our own scenarios, we build our own destiny, if she didn't exist ten years ago, why is she now so important?

I was observing this strange game!

Me, Ruben, the big preacher, philosopher, leader who could give many spiritual advises in his youth, and guide the masses through their sufferings, now, had to put up his own Life onto the Lilith's stage, his own Heart under the grounding wheel, enter the endless circle of suffering Me.

The suffering was suffocating Me.

I screamed hitting the boundaries of my own skin, I screamed trying to be heard in this world of faceless faces walking on this Earth not noticing anybody, screaming a silent scream that tore apart my insides. Death no longer scared me, it was the emptiness of Life...

At that point I knew, no matter what the circumstances, no matter what Life gives, we still experience deep luck of love, deep luck of fate and deep luck of God. The question 'why me?' is irrelevant, it is for the weak ones, for the ones who don't have the Wisdom to see the universality of this crazy feeling...

Diving deeper into my own fixation of separateness, into my own scream, I saw myself at five, at twenty, at forty, 100s of years ago, and far down the path of the future, and God was always there, and she, Lilith, was always there.

My mother stood next to the window every morning looking at a house across the river, wishing to be a part of its household, dreaming and praying for a new life that will bring her happiness. I saw her wish come true, moving to the house of my father, now standing next to the window of the new home, looking at the old house, every single day, waiting for the sunrise with the same thought: I wish that I can go back in time and be in the house across the river where I was happy.

Seeing my father madly in love, ready to kill and die for the chosen one, always leaving her every time she completely gave him her heart and I saw him suffering lonely surrounded with strangers from lack of love.

I saw lovers who were not meant to be together because their families wouldn't allow it or they lived in different places or because of the age difference or difference in class, or because they were separated by wars, poverty, disease and I saw them dying of broken hearts.

In the midst of the play, of my own theatre, my own game, the scenario continued with unlimited number of roles.

As long as the belief is: we need suffering to grow, the world will be suffering and the belief will be limiting...

Stumble in despair, search for her, in the branches of the trees hanging over the cliff, asking: why? why suffering? My misery needed an answer.

This was definitely not a mistake nor a coincidence, God as a perfect conductor invented Lilith for a reason!

The vision came back to haunt me. This time I was in my own body sometime in the future. Inside, there were only broken bones.

There has been nothing before and there will be nothing after this feeling of deep sadness. Lilith voice said.

My face disappeared within the white mist, I was a dead man walking, with the head in my hands, puzzled why everybody is looking. I was a walking pain.

You are the man who once had everything, Lilith said, a warm home, an exciting mission, a powerful church, your friends, your loved one, they all disappeared, at once.

I turned around, I thought I've heard God laughing.

If I wanted money, I got it, piles of it. If I wanted power, people were at my feet, wanted me to like them, wanted me to nod in an approval, wanted me to send a blessing, wanted me to smile. If I wanted love, I got a most amazing woman falling in love with me, if I wanted Knowledge, it accumulated within my mind to excite the followers. I had everything and I had a freedom to choose. All through my life I had a freedom to choose...

My Soul was in pain.

Today with no love, no friends, no mission or future to call my-own, I heard my thoughts echoing through the valley.

The same people that once admired me because I looked wise and powerful, self-confident and strong, despised me, and asked me to go back to the world of slander, the world of confusion that was full of misconceptions of what the Truth is.

Walking alone through the mazes of unknown streets, lost in my thoughts I was looking for the meaning of life.

The belief in God did not offer comfort, why, why would a soul choose a life of separation, why would we constantly come back to suffering?

Suddenly a child was trapped inside of me, crying. My heart bled listening its screams. The little one was hurt and there was nothing I could do to stop its anguish. The rain within the depths of my heart smelled of the fear invading. You all probably are familiar with the sound of a child crying! The scream that is complete, frantically devoted to its core, expressing the pain of the whole mankind. The cause is lost, the reason gone, just the cry stays, merging with the screams of many unconscious us.

Shhhhhhhhh, my dear one, some tried to console it, shhhhhhhhh. Gentle whispers, shhhhhhhh, our loved one, shhhhhhhhh, the voices offered hope, warmth and love. We'll secure your little body, calm your little mind, guard you from attacks of evil, we'll give you colours, scents and the feel of the mother's protected womb. Calm down, our dear one, calm down, they tried. All for nothing... The child's cry lasted for hours. Hours...

After I stopped crying I realised how much the child within me needed this cry drowning within the spheres of unassuming.

I understood – the humankind need to suffer is very deep.

I meditated – the human need to love is very deep.

A thought appeared from the depth of the darkness: isn't that what it is all about?

Love gives, just like a flower would, giving its fragrance to the world, completely, unassuming, unconditionally. Ama danced through her love game singing.

But now, when Ama is gone, just a thought of her name brought back an instant sharp physical pain.

A thought crept into my mind, a thought planted within me all these years of priesthood: the pain is not useless, remember, it has its own purpose, it has within a secret of remembering. When an arrow goes deep into the flesh the pain makes you more alert, more conscious, when you start bleeding you become aware of others, your wisdom deepens, your soul to soul contact with people deepens. You have decided to leave the Garden of Eden, life there was too easy, too comfortable, you were not alert.

I shook off this thought, I could almost hear Ama laughing hearing these words 'and your understanding gets more and more profound but it is still very childlike'.

Just remembering her voice, brought back a glimpse of an intention, today so far, almost forgotten, that slept deep within my Being, the urge for Light, Light found within, Light that in our ignorance and desperation we try to find outside.

'Stop the dance for a moment',

'When you stop the dance, and turn your eyes inwards, for a moment, a miracle happens! Entering the sound of Silence, the pain disappears.'

Shaken out of my dream state, observing my little stage, I saw the pain as a companion constantly seeking attention, appearing and disappearing, becoming the centre illusion, whenever I let it Be.

If suffering does not exist, happiness would not be that sweet, a thought came to my mind. If we are never thirsty we will never experience the beauty of water. Suffering teaches us compassion.

I was not entirely sure were these my thoughts or thoughts of the humankind that knows of no other way...

Within the sound of waves breaking underneath my feet, I could again hear Ama laughing. These were words of Ruben who is consoling his flock.

But there surely is another way, I screamed into nothingness.
When did all of this begin? I cannot see the end of it, but there must have been a beginning!

A bird flitted from my sight taking with it a thought of suffering that was with me since the beginning of time.

'The moment has never happened', I've heard Ama,

'It is all an illusion,

Its birth, its existence, its reality,

All of it is in your head.'

My imaginary conversation with Ama was the only sane corner within the alley of my misery, so I dived into it *with a spark of hope as a drank-man would faced with a medusa's deadly glow.*

You were in love with me yesterday, you are in pain today and you will not remember me tomorrow.

I will always remember you, I stopped her!

Don't say always, she said, always does not exist...

Always, always, always, I repeated my little mantra.

Nothing is static, you are that endless combination of your thoughts, feelings, cells. In reality, with no static you, we just have a series of memories implanted within your brain that outlived the phenomenon of forgiveness, just a perception of you that lives in your own head.

Will you remember me?

If I paint your image and frame it, the reality of that image will be gone even before you completely become aware of its existence.

You are being cruel to me! I stopped her. Is that because I left you?

You live in our past and in the thought of the future we will never have and these two you call yourselves, but both of them are not real. Ama was correct.

I love you and that reality is the only reality I feel right now! I left you and the life I chose is the life I cannot recognise or accept.

She wiped a tear rolling down my cheek releasing it into a crack of a stone, where it formed a crystal millions of years later that hid a story of my lost and never-again-to-be-found love.

She took my hand delivering me onto the journey of my past.

Come with me now into the narrow streets of Macao contemplating Life and our original sin, separation from God. Come with me into the head of a young Ruben, the head of a priest that has just moved to China, some decades ago, before he fell in love and before he left his beloved.

Come with me into your past, in hope to find the key, and in some future lives avoid my bitter cup. Enter his story once again, but be aware, that we could be a part of any man's life, going into any other century or place, following the destiny, walking on our journey towards the Truth.

I saw a bird that fell out of its nest, just born, beautiful in its fragility and it died under a tree, all in front of my eyes. I saw it dying... Giving birth and being born is painful; ageing as decaying surrounds us, nature is cruel...

Ruben smelled the air, he felt the spring in his lungs. He felt the first sun rays caressing his forehead.

Does the grass know that it is dying and does a bird suffer when her baby falls out of the nest? We, humans, give it much more strength and much more importance than any other living creature.

Being conscious of how temporary Life is, we suffer, contemplated Ruben.

We all pass through the same movements: birth, growth, wish to procreate, wish to socialise, decay, death, the only thing that separates us from other living beings on this little planet Earth is that we are conscious of what is happening to us. We are conscious of the Life's game, of the eternal spiral and this causes us pain. Yet, the same consciousness accelerates our search for the higher meanings in Life.

The same consciousness gives us strength to continue our journey until the final goal is met, our merge with God.

Ruben took the fragile body into his hands creating a little tomb for the dead bird. Its body still looked perfect mirroring the miracle of Life.

Looking at it, Ruben saw the Universe as a vast organism that breathes and develops, with its parts moving and interacting, creating a mysterious resonance that constantly changes.

He buried the little bones covered in feathers, blessed it with leaves, leaving behind just a few traces of a human interaction with Nature, that wind will disperse returning to the perfect balance. The Death will in no time become invisible to the eyes of passers-by.

We all dance within this stage, within Life, thought Ruben, still kneeling down after his little funeral, *and while dancing, we seek to understand this web of energies. Is this the essence of our Work? This understanding of Life and Death?*

Looking up, through the trees, into the clouds, he couldn't help feeling, that someone is watching attentively...

Ever desire-less, one can see the mystery
Ever desiring, one can see the manifestations
Tao Te Ching

A Man Training to Be

The air smelled of pine. Cool air covered my skin and the moon looked at me, talking – in signs. Lost in the movements, I was seeking the End. Looking within...

Alone, in the presence of others, all my life I walked the dream of Life.

Dressed in white with a transparent body of Light, a vision appeared, a vision of my enlightenment. A wind follows Her subtle, gentle being, she is the Master of the surrounding waters. She took my Heart and the same Heart painfully trapped by my Mind, was now released, re-birthing in Joy filled with strength and beauty.

A sign engraved on my forehead set me apart from the islands of man. The sign carried the question and the answer, shining as a star marking the beginning and the end of the journey.

She said: At the beginning there was a word, word and a sound.

God was that sound.

Sound was a vibration and vibration was energy.

Life decided to move away from God.

God has decided to create Life.

And it all started materialising, here, on Earth.

Cells, living organisms, grass, trees, enlightened trees, beautiful old trees that concurred death able to live for thousands of years.

Cells, living organism, forming into animals, evolving into humans that try to break the circle of life and death through consciousness.

Identifying with the separateness created an isolation of units and an illusion of division from Life.

Consciousness opened eyes to suffering, opening a channel for accelerated growth and the everlasting wish to break the circle of Life and merge with God – NOW.

From stone to stone, a walk became a run, Orion smiled at me from above. The visibility was low, I felt the confidence building protected by the stars and the Moon light hidden behind a cloud in the distance. The spirits of Water, Stone and Wind accompanied me. The strength of Earth supported me through the sounds and whispers of the night. Very soon, a little goat within me found its way following the inborn trust in its own steps. From stone to stone, with every breath, closer and closer to the sea. I jumped over the water pools, avoiding the cracks, animals, worlds of unknown, caves of damp and darkness, walking the edge, closer and closer to the sea.

All through my journey, the call stayed clear, coming from the depths of waters, merge with One!

We know you, we belong to the same gap in Time. Our heartbeat connects with yours. You are given the chance to sail the wave of our truth and move the boundaries between the understandings of two realities. You have seen the birth of Venus. The foam's crystal white, from the depth of the sea, through stone and wind, the shell emerged caring the beauty of the pearl in its hidden core. Opening to you, disclosing secrets of birth and death in its golden transformation, She unfolded.

In between reality and dreams there was a World that just a few with open eyes can enter. I trusted Orion and Earth carried over the rocks into that world of altered realities. Merged with Life I understood the power within me.

The Sea has given me its code. Blue and endless, it surrounded the whole of my being, it entered my core. Running through my blood, spiralling my skin, moving within the cells of my body, it gave me the ability to become It. I could finally communicate with Life understanding its movements, breathing, the process of evolution, the emergence of cells, the process of growth.

Merging with God, it was easy to live Love for all the creatures, to know Love as unchangeable within. I entered the Lotus of Heart.

Still in trance, experiencing minutes as hours, days, eons, I've heard Her voice:

'May the clarity of my vision guide you, for I am a part of you.
May my breath become your breath and fill you with Life.
May my words find a place of truth within your heart.

Allow my love enter your body with the gift of Life.
May you become this most precious gift; your Divine Nature.
Through our time together, may you know Yourself.
In that knowing, may you find your true home, the God within.'

Finally alone with no roles to play. I was the loneliest person on Earth and completely fulfilled.

At the beginning of the journey.

She was with me many times since, in dreams guiding my Soul gently and firmly, always closer to One.

On my journey, 5 years later, sitting around the fire during one cold winter day, I heard a story that best described Her nature, her name was Nirvana.
Is there such a thing as wind?
Of course there is, came the reply.
What is its colour, its shape, its thickness?
It has no colour or shape or thickness.
Can one touch it and can it be shown?
No, it cannot be touched and it cannot be shown.
If it cannot be shown, how do you know it exists?

I am positive it exists, even if it cannot be seen.
Nirvana is like that.
It cannot be touched, or seen.
But we are positive it exists.

Last time I saw Her, was the night before I died, again in my dream, She came to visit. Compassion personified, free from sorrow and completely radiant, she kissed me, giving me a sign, allowing me to come with Her into Unknown. My mission on Earth was fulfilled, I was ready to leave this realm realised and peaceful.

V.I.T.R.I.O.L.

Visita
Interiora
Terrae
Ractificando
Invenies
Occultum
Lapidem

Visita Interiora Terrae Ractificando Invenies Occultum Lapidem

Fire, Water, and Air.
Being, Knowledge, and Bliss.

Sulphur is a male fiery manifestation of the Universe, it is activity, desire, the Rajas that is seen as energy, excitement, fire, brilliance, restlessness, the swift and creative, it is the initiative of all Being. It represents sudden and violent but impermanent activity. If it persists for too long, it will burn and destroy.

Mercury is fluidity, intelligence and power of transmission, it is the energy sent forth. Represents the Wisdom, the Will, the Word of creation whose speech is silence, it is Satva that is calm, intelligence and balance. It represents creation in all forms. Unexpected, he unsettles any established idea.

Salt is the vehicle of two forms of energy. The formula of our Universe is Love governed by Venus. She combines the highest spiritual with the lowest material qualities – Love materialised on Earth. Born in water, from mud, she bears the lotus. Salt is inactive principle of Nature and it is seen as Tamas – darkness, inertia, sloth, ignorance, death. It is matter that must be energised by Sulphur to maintain the equilibrium.

Life has emerged as an interplay of the three elements and as such is in a state of continuous change. Nothing can remain in any phase where one state is predominant. Three elements flow into each other, reward of an effort is peace that ultimately sinks into the original inertia.

In the process of creation, the Black King is marrying the White Queen, the male and the female principle in Nature are merging. The energy sent forth through the Will, is penetrating the female aspects of the Universe to create Life. The formulation of any idea creates its opposite and this preserves the equilibrium of the Universe. The opposites are equal and they manifest in various forms, Sun and Moon, Light and Darkness, Fire and Water, Air and Earth, Spirit and Soul. The result of the marriage is the Orphic egg that is the essence of Life – the colour of egg is grey. It is capable of taking any possible form.

Any Thought merging from Life becomes a Separation and it can be balanced if it is married with its Contradiction. The merge brings equilibrium, the white woman now has a black head, the black king a white one, the fire burns up the water and the water extinguish the fire to be harmoniously mingled at the end. Below the Abyss, contradiction is division, but above the Abyss, contradiction is Unity.

The formula of continued life is death.
The formula of ascending above the Abyss is resurrection.
In the process of transformation the life form from the Orphic egg has to die to be reborn again.

The spirit, as mighty fire descends and connects itself with now completely purified soul giving re-birth to the divine man. The King and the Queen are resurrected to give a birth to the new body. The merge, this time, led by conscious effort, brings love and joy into heart of man, creating the light that will destroy and re-create the world.

Within the earth's womb each metal grows slowly developing and transforming into its perfection, its highest manifestation – gold. Nature and God are striving towards perfection, everything moves towards One. Just as human strive to become fully conscious, so all the metals strive to reach their purest state – gold.

Gold by its nature does not rot or decay and that is why it is the most precious. Gold is not receptive to oxygen that is breath of life for living organisms.

Visita interiora terrae ractificando invenies occultum lapidem.

Visit the interior parts of the Earth: by rectification you shall find the hidden stone.

V.I.T.R.I.O.L. is a balanced combination of the three alchemical principles, Sulphur, Mercury and Salt.
Through the rectification the new life is created.
Through the rectification Spirit and Soul merge creating a new body, a new divine personality.
Through the rectification life is correctly led in the path of the True Will. Love is the law, Love controlled by Will.

Through the rectification True Will springs from within as a fountain of Light and the flow of Love leads into the Ocean of Life.

Through the rectification action brings Perfection that is Silence and every form of energy is directed, applied with integrity to the full satisfaction of its destiny.

when a particle and antiparticle touch
they both disappear in a burst
of gamma radiation
that generates huge amount of energy...
can this be Love?

Nuit

About the Author

Nataša Pantović, MSc Economics, is Serbian / Maltese Novelist, Management Consultant, Adoptive Parent, and Ancient World's Consciousness Researcher.

Published Author since 1991, with a legal self-help book on Cooperative Law published in two editions by Poslovni Biro, Yugoslavia. Since joining the AoL team has authored and co-authored 9 AoL Books.

The early eMalta years saw a heavy investment by Government in its ICT infrastructure to transform Malta into an Information Society. As Management Consultant working within the MEU, in the Office of Prime Minister, Nataša worked on large number of management and HR consulting projects throughout the various Ministries / Government Institutions.

While heading a large UK IT company (Crimsonwing, later KPMG) that has set-up its operations in Malta, she was in charge of its Management Consultancy, Training, and Business Development, expanding the company's markets in Europe, and has been invited by Malta Enterprise, to promote Malta as a European near-shore IT outsourcing destination. As a woman, and an IT Executive, travelling around our little planet, her memory recalls many venues in London, Cardif, Manchester, Milan, Brussels, Rome, Amsterdam, presenting the company's large UK IT case studies (Safeway, Banks, etc.) while at the same time promoting Malta IT, but the most impressive was the Euro-Med Summit in Marseille (France) where Nataša was a Guest Speaker in an Experts Panel Discussion addressing Ministers and Business Heads from around the Euro-Med region with the Presentation Strategies for Growth in the Euro-Med Region Euro-Mediterranean Business Summit 2006.

After helping Father George build a school in a remote area of Ethiopia, Nuit entered the most amazing world of parenting adopting two kids from Ethiopia as a single mum. Nuit left her Management Consultancy job to follow this amazing journey into the parenthood. At the moment she says that her kids are actively teaching her how to be a more loving, mindful and conscious parent. Ema and Andrej love and train basketball, play music, act within a Music Theatre Group and were Chess Champions of Malta.

Nataša has travelled through more than 50 countries and lived in 5: UK, New Zealand, Holland, Serbia and Malta. As a volunteer she organized six Body Mind Spirit Festivals in Malta, an International Vegetarian Festival, a Children Festival, and 10 days Temples Conference. She regularly writes about variety of self-development topics with Times of Malta.

A-Ma or Playing the Glass Bead Game with Pythagoras
© Artof4Elements / March 2016

All rights reserved

No part of this book may be reproduced or
Transmitted in any form or by any means
Without permission in writing from the publisher.
For information address: Artof4Elements

ISBN 978-9995754198

Pantović Nataša, A-Ma or Playing the Glass Bead Game with Pythagoras
-English-

Published by artof4Elements
4, Holly Wood, St. Albert Street, Gzira GZR1157,
Malta

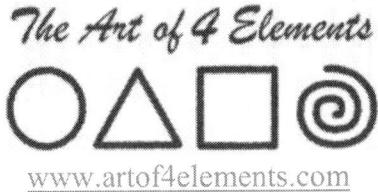

www.artof4elements.com

Printed in Poland
by Amazon Fulfillment
Poland Sp. z o.o., Wrocław

79655341R00122